Old Bones

By the same author

Pick Up

Old Bones

J. A. O'Brien

ROBERT HALE · LONDON

© J. A. O'Brien 2008
First published in Great Britain 2008

ISBN 978-0-7090-8537-9

Robert Hale Limited
Clerkenwell House
Clerkenwell Green
London EC1R 0HT

www.halebooks.com

The right of James O'Brien to be identified as
author of this work has been asserted by him
in accordance with the Copyright, Designs and
Patents Act 1988

2 4 6 8 10 9 7 5 3 1

Typeset in 11½/17pt Palatino
by Derek Doyle & Associates, Shaw Heath
Printed and bound in Great Britain
by Biddles Limited, King's Lynn

Dedicated with love and affection to my son Michael.

CHAPTER ONE

'Old bones, Speckle!'

'Pardon, sir?' said Sally Speckle.

'Skeleton. Thatcher's Lot. Well, what're you waiting for? Off with you, Inspector. DS Lukeson's already in situ.'

The phone went dead, just as Sally Speckle was about to remind Chief Superintendent Frank 'Sermon' Doyle that she was on leave. Though Doyle had earned his nickname for his long-windedness (particularly when it came to the need to curb overtime), when it suited him, as it obviously had just now, he could also show his talent for brevity. Then 'Sermon' Doyle had a simple system. He said hop and you jumped.

DS Andy Lukeson's words drifted back to Speckle.

'Give it time, Sally,' had been Lukeson's advice. 'They'll come round when they realize that you're a copper through and through. Every DI, grad or trad, has to earn respect.'

Lukeson's comments had come at a particularly low point in her first case (this skeleton in Thatcher's Lot, if murder had been done, would be only her second murder investigation) when she had thought about quitting the force because she had doubted that she would solve the Pick Up case, as the press had termed it, officially case number T/C34621/L in which T stood for Tettle (Anne Tettle) and C stood for Collins (Brenda Collins), both done to death by a very cunning killer – L for Loston. And the second reason for her quitting had been the tension her promotion from Administration to CID had caused with her fellow officers. She was a graddie, the unflattering name given to officers who had entered the force through the graduate programme and were seen as being favoured by senior management, whose brainchild the scheme had been, above the traditional copper, to ensure that the programme was seen to be a success. And now, even after the successful conclusion of the Pick Up case, she had not been wholly accepted into the ranks of *real* detective inspectors.

Thatcher's Lot, about three miles out of Loston, was an oddity. Part bog, part rock and part wood, it was like a misplaced chunk of Yorkshire moor that should be returned before someone missed it and got stroppy about it. A mist which had never fully lifted felt like ghostly wet fingers on Speckle's face.

Thatcher's Lot was a gloomy place.

DS Andy Lukeson detached himself from a man and

woman he was talking to (the man was holding a metal detector) and came to meet her, his footsteps on the spongy turf akin to the sucking sound of a tooth being pulled.

'The metal detector found the grave,' he said. 'There's a shoulder-bag strap with a brass ring in the grave. That's what he must have picked up.'

'How old do you think this skeleton is, Andy?'

Lukeson shrugged. 'Your guess is as good as mine. We'll have to await greater minds than ours to tell us that. The strap would normally have two brass rings but it was cut, leaving only one ring. If the cut end was drawn through the ringed end it would have made a very effective ligature.'

'Male or female?'

'It's just a skull and a couple of ribs at the moment, but I reckon that the size of the skull would suggest a female or perhaps a teenage boy?' He nodded in the direction of the man and woman he had been talking with when she had arrived. 'Fred and Ettie White.'

To the right of where the Whites were, there was a shallow hole in the ground over which a white tent had been placed. Blue and white tape, securing the patch, was wound from tree to tree to mark the boundaries of the crime scene.

'Better introduce me, then,' Speckle said.

As Speckle and Lukeson approached, Fred White said, 'Now remember, Ettie. Nothing about that gold watch I found here. Understood?'

'That was ages ago.'

'Don't matter. Coppers are coppers. They'll want to know why I didn't hand it in for the owner to be found, won't they?'

'If you flogged it and bought me that new kitchen I been looking for, you wouldn't have it for them to take now, would you, Fred White?'

'It's me nest egg, isn't it? Now just be careful, OK?'

'Mr and Mrs White,' Lukeson introduced, coming up to the Whites. 'DI Speckle.'

'It was a terrible shock, I can tell you, Inspector,' said Ettie White.

'I'm sure it was, Mrs White,' Speckle sympathized.

'Any idea who it is?'

'Early days yet.'

'Of course. There ain't much you can do with a load of old bones, is there?' Fred White said. 'Have to wait for them foresic johnnies to tell you, don't you?'

'Forensic,' Ettie said.

'What?'

'Forensic,' Ettie White repeated, as if trying to get through to an idiot.

'That's what I just said,' Fred responded, argumentatively.

'No, you didn't. You said foresic. No "n", you see.' She spelled it out. 'F-O-R-E-N-S-I-C.'

'Bollocks!' Fred spat.

'You watch your tongue, Fred White,' Ettie rebuked her husband.

Fred White turned his attention to Sally Speckle.

'Do Ettie and me have to hang round for much longer?'

Sally Speckle looked to Lukeson.

'We have a brief statement,' he said.

'We'll not keep you, then,' the DI told the Whites. 'We can send someone round to get more detailed statements later on.'

'Don't know what more me and Ettie can tell you, Inspector,' Fred White grumbled. He pulled the collar of his anorak up round him. 'I'll be glad to see the back of this place, I can tell you, Inspector.'

'As will I. Do you need a lift?'

'No. I brought the car. It's parked near the entrance to the wood.'

'Drive safely, then. And thank you.'

'For nothing, I'm sure,' Ettie White said.

As they walked away the argument about *foresic* and *forensics* started up again.

'I think poor old Fred is in for a right bollocking,' Lukeson said, with a wry smile, watching Ettie White's mouth opening and closing like a stranded fish, Fred not getting a word in.

'Let's go and look at the remains, shall we?' A moment later, looking into the shallow grave, Speckle observed. 'Not much to do really, until we have an idea of how long the skeleton's been there. At that point we can start to check on missing persons from around that time.'

Rain began to fall.

'Shit! the DI swore, looking up at the milling rainclouds, driven by a rising wind. 'Tell me it's not going to rain through this investigation as it did in the Tettle and Collins murders.'

'The weather forecast was for passing showers.'

'I should have worn an anorak with a hood.' Speckle ran her fingers through her auburn hair. 'I've just paid forty quid to have this lot done.'

'Suits you,' Lukeson said.

'Don't bother,' she said. 'You didn't even notice.'

CHAPTER TWO

'OK, settle down,' said DI Sally Speckle on entering the briefing room, as laughter erupted on the punchline of DC Charlie Johnson's joke about, from what she could gather, an ant who fancied an elephant. She looked around at the familiar faces of the team she had assembled for her first case, and was pleased that that should make for quick progress, in that each member of the team's capabilites were known to her and DS Andy Lukeson and each other, which would make it possible to match assignments to skills.

Some officers preferred field work and were unhappy messing about with computers and databases, while others found their true niche in such activities. Assigned a task which held little or no interest for an officer often meant slovenly work which could greatly hamper an investigation or, in the extreme, put at risk a successful conclusion. The exception this time round was PC Roger Bennett. And, if Sally Speckle was to be absolutely honest with herself, she was somewhat relieved at his not being there, although she would in no way have wished that the circumstances which led to his absence (selling information to Nick Hornby the TV reporter to pay off his gambling debts) had come about. 'Now for the nitty-gritty.' Speckle held up the thin report of the initial findings to kick-start the investigation. 'What nitty-gritty there is so far. The skeleton is that of a young female. Put at, as it stands, somewhere between fifteen and twenty. Not pinpoint accuracy, I know,' she said on hearing a collective groan, 'but we can't hang about waiting for a battery of tests on the skeleton to give us a definite age. Any work done now should be of benefit if we haven't caught the killer before then. So fifteen to twenty is our guideline. Estimated height is about five feet eight inches—'

'Brussels will have you by the short and curlies if you don't use metres and centimetres, boss,' Charlie Johnson said. 'Next we'll be having pounds and ounces!'

When the laughter faded, DI Sally Speckle continued:

'The remains have lain in the ground for approximately five years. So we start with missing persons from around that time, between fifteen and twenty years old. The teeth had been first class and expensively maintained. So when that list is drawn up, names with an address to match the cost of such dental care will be a natural starting point. Cause of death in this instance will probably remain a mystery, but it is reasonably safe to assume that a shoulder-bag strap, I'd imagine – one of those bags that you could hide a battleship in – found under what would have been the neck of the victim was used to strangle her. The strap has one large brass ring' – she passed a photograph of the strap around – 'when clearly it should have had two matching rings. This is probably the murder weapon.' Sally Speckle took a replica strap, cut off one ring and put the end of the strap through the other ring which she then pulled through. 'It makes a very effective ligature. The skeleton in the main is complete. The grave where the skeleton was found is still being sifted through, but that will be a long and slow process. Dental records might identify the woman. So we'll concentrate first on dentists in and around Loston. Hopefully we'll strike lucky and be able to ID her quickly. Failing that, we will, of course, seek DNA samples from the families of those listed as missing, of which I'm hoping there won't be too many. Now, we'll need everyone to be at their diplomatic best. We'll be raising ghosts and opening old wounds for a lot of people. The nasal sill tells us that the skull is caucasoid.' Sally Speckle grinned. 'Which, to all ranks lower than a DI, who know about these things, means that the woman was white. So we're only interested in white women who went missing in the region of five years ago.

'We made a good team last time. And this time should be no different. DS Lukeson will give you your assignments.'

Sally Speckle felt a return of the nervousness she had experienced on her first murder investigation. She would once more be under scrutiny, and all the old problems of graddies (graduate coppers) versus trads (traditional coppers) would come to the fore.

Speckle's first murder investigation had been one during which she had had many doubts about the wisdom of having allowed herself to be pushed into becoming a detective inspector in CID before what other officers thought was her time, which meant promotion gained by hard slog rather than being fast-tracked through the graduate recruitment programme beloved of senior officers and Whitehall Mandarins who reckoned that as an employment opportunity, the police needed to shed its more downmarket image and compete for the annual crop of graduates. The programme had certainly been responsible for a wide divergence between types of officers and approaches, but whether the police had become more efficient was something that the jury was still out on, because the programme had created a lot of divisions and grudges that, in a business that depended greatly on cooperation to achieve results, may not have been the brilliant idea it had once seemed to be. She had, due to a successful conclusion to the Pick Up case, gained more acceptance from colleagues. But she was under no illusions: she would have to show her investigative mettle more than once to gain full acceptance. One colleague had stated it so succinctly: 'As me old gran used to say, one swallow doesn't make a summer.' Without the team she was lucky to have led, she would probably have scampered back to the safety of life outside the police. And particularly without one man in that team – Detective Sergeant Andy Lukeson.

'A female killer, then, boss?' DC Helen Rochester pondered. 'Shoulder-bag strap as a murder weapon.'

'Don't let's start out with any preconceived ideas,' Speckle cautioned. 'A closed mind makes for blinkered vision.'

'Anything that can be gleaned from the strap?' DC Charlie Johnson asked.

'The lab is working on it. The problem is, the bag is of the cheap mass-produced variety. So I wouldn't hold my breath. If there is something to be discovered, it will take a hell of a long time, I reckon.'

'Any prints, maybe on the buckle?' WPC Anne Fenning asked. 'Brass buckles are good for prints.'

'Nothing obvious. After five years that would be unlikely,' Speckle said. 'But all the wizardry of modern science is being brought to bear. But, again, I wouldn't hold my breath, Anne.'

'Pretty silly, that. Leaving the murder weapon behind,' WPC Sue Blake said. 'It would have been as easy for the killer to take it away.'

'Silliness, or perhaps arrogance?' Andy Lukeson suggested.

'Panic?' WPC Anne Fenning speculated.

'Doubt it,' Lukeson said. 'You'd have to be a pretty cool customer to bury a body. Not given to panic. Besides, I shouldn't imagine that the killer would do the spadework in broad daylight. The view in a wood is limited. Someone could pop up at any second. My guess would be that if the killer struck in daylight, he hid the body and came back later when it was dark. And, of course, we have no evidence to say that the woman was murdered where she was buried.'

'Strangling is more a man thing, isn't it?' PC Brian Scuttle said. 'I mean, it takes quite a bit of effort to strangle a struggling victim.'

DC Charlie Johnson chuckled. 'Strangled many, have you, Brian?'

'Piss-take aside,' Speckle said, 'Brian has a vaild point. But I reckon that a very fit woman could be our killer. Andy?'

'I reckon,' Lukeson concurred.

'OK,' the DI said, clapping her hands like a schoolmarm. 'To kick off, we'll need that list of missing persons. Once we have that info we'll form interview teams.'

'Andy. A moment, please.'

Lukeson followed Speckle to her office.

'I've just had a phone call. PC Roger Bennett is unconscious in ICU in Loston Hospital. Some of those friends he owed money to seem to have run out of patience.'

'I thought he was over his gambling problem?'

'He was doing well, but he must have gone back to old habits. I thought as much. He's been missing for the last week. Didn't report. He must have been in hiding.'

'Rotten bastards!'

Speckle had informed Lukeson at the end of the Pick Up case of Bennett's addiction to gambling. 'He was found in an alley connecting Grey's Quay to Easton Way.' She sighed. 'I thought he was doing really well in the rehab programme.'

When Bennett had confessed his treachery in flogging information to Nick Hornby the TV reporter (which had caused considerable anger and loss of face to Speckle in a TV interview during the Pick Up case), Sally Speckle had held back on disciplinary procedures, provided that Bennett sought help for his problem. It was a decent thing to do. Other DIs would have had his scalp there and then for a whole lot less than the embarrassment he had caused his DI and the potential damage to the investigation his activities might have caused.

'Will he pull through?' Lukeson asked, genuinely concerned.

'He's in a pretty bad way, Andy.'

'Shouldn't we tell the others?'

'I'm not sure. Wouldn't it preoccupy them, at a time when they'll need their full concentration?'

'It won't be a secret for long,' Lukeson warned. 'And as

a team they'll not take to it kindly if they hear about Roger Bennett from someone else.'

'I suppose you're right. I'll leave it to you, shall I?'

'It would be much better coming from you,' Lukeson opined. 'After all, you're the boss.'

'Flatterer. But you're right, of course.'

'But,' Lukeson went on, 'it will probably hold until we get that list we're looking for. Nothing as detrimental to a good investigation as a disjointed start.'

DI Sally Speckle smiled. 'What would I do without you, Sergeant?'

Her mind went back to when they had charged the killer in the Pick Up case, and she had shared a celebratory drink with Andy Lukeson. In fact, they had shared more than one drink and had arrived back at her flat pretty sloshed and in a silly mood that had almost ended passionately, before good sense prevailed. Since then, she had often wondered what might have been the outcome, short and long term, had that one fumbling kiss become anything more. Andy Lukeson had never mentioned it. Neither had she. But that frenetic moment had lain between them since, unresolved and unspoken of. A time or two she had been tempted to clear the air, but had never had the courage to do so. She could not help wondering if Andy had completely forgotten about it. Or, like her, had he too often wanted to pick over the bones of that almost passionate encounter?

CHAPTER THREE

DC Helen Rochester handed Dl Sally Speckle the list of names of missing females from the search of the database which WPC Anne Fenning had drawn up, along with the case files. The list consisted of six names:

Ava Black
Elinor Roebuck
Linda Wright
Christine Walsh
Susan Finch
Alison Crowe

'A mixed bunch,' Rochester commented. 'These two' – the DC encircled in red the names of Elinor Roebuck and Susan Finch – 'are the most likely to have had expensive dental treatment. Roebuck had an address in Loston's stockbroker belt, where a million pounds would not go very far in purchasing a property. Finch had lived in a village a couple of miles out of Loston on the Brigham Road and an equally upmarket location.'

'Interesting,' Speckle said. 'Roebuck and Finch went missing within days of each other in July. Roebuck first, on a Thursday, and Finch on Saturday. Wonder if Finch and Roebuck knew each other? And if they did, were they friends or enemies?'

'You think that if they were enemies, Finch might have offed Roebuck on Thursday and did a runner on Saturday?'

'I think it's a door we could let open, Helen.'

The other names on the list were from less impressive addresses and the attached files were less bulky than those of Roebuck and Finch, indicating that more effort had gone into finding the upmarket women than those from a less exalted background, the conclusion being (perhaps wrongly) that the parents of a woman like Christine Walsh who lived in a council flat were less worthy to have their daughter found than Roebuck and Finch's parents were. Frank Walsh, a truck driver, was unlikely to be found on Loston's exclusive golf club exchanging funny handshakes. Fact? Or prejudice born of her desire to change the world and the system, as she supposed was the mission every copper started out with before the realization hit them that no matter how hard they tried, when they finally reached their pension, the system, if it had changed at all, would have changed more for the privileged few than the downtrodden masses. And that's when despondency set in and the flame of enthusiasm dimmed, and one fitted neatly in or was quickly sidelined and mentioned of as being *difficult*.

The names of the investigating officers were interesting. DI Jack Allen, who had led the search for Elinor Roebuck was now in Traffic (at best a sideways move, at worst a demotion, depending on whether one considered the glass half empty or half full). DI Harry Chalke (older than Allen) had taken early retirement shortly after the search for Susan Finch ran out of steam. And the other officers, all detective sergeants with the exception of one who was a DCI at the time, were still on the force, two of whom had gained promotion to DI and one, DCI Frank Doyle, to chief superintendent – CS Frank 'Sermon' Doyle. One could draw obvious conclusions, Speckle thought. However, the obvious was not always right, as every raw recruit to the police soon learned.

Based on the estimated height of the skeleton, Speckle put a question mark after two names – Ava Black, who was five foot four inches, and Alison Crowe, who was five foot two inches. 'We'll begin with the others,' she said. 'It says here that Christine Walsh disappeared after attending a hospital clinic. Do we know what kind of clinic it was.'

'Couldn't find any mention of it.'

Speckle checked the name of the investigating officer and found that it was a DCI Frank Doyle.

'Shit.'

'What?'

Speckle turned the file towards Rochester, her finger on the name of the investigating officer.

'That Doyle?' Helen Rochester asked, pointing at the ceiling.

'Yes.'

'Shit again, boss!'

DI Sally Speckle picked up the phone and punched out Doyle's extension number.

'Yes?' Doyle barked down the line.

Speckle crossed her fingers. 'Sir, Sally Speckle here.'

'I'm rather busy right now, Speckle. It's this bloody overtime budget. Running this place is costing more than the war in . . . wherever we are now.'

'This shouldn't take long, sir.'

'Go on, then. Out with it.'

'It's about this skeleton that was found, sir.'

'Give me good news, Speckle. Tell me that it's the remains of a Roman general and it's none of our concern.'

'Sorry, sir. It's only been about five years in the ground. Prelim estimate, of course.'

'That's the Roman general out, then. Well, I can't stay on the end of this phone all bloody morning, Speckle. Get to the point.'

DC Helen Rochester winced. Doyle's booming voice was making her privy to the entire conversation.

'I have a list of women who disappeared around five

years ago—'

'Many, are there?'

'Six. But based on the estimated height of the remains, we've put two on the back-burner. That leaves four.'

'I *can* count, Inspector,' Doyle said sarcastically. 'Only too bloody well. If I couldn't these overtime figures might not be as alarming.'

'The thing is, sir. You were the investigating officer on one of these cases—'

'Five years ago? That would be Christine Walsh. Right?'

'Yes.'

'What about it?' Doyle enquired brusquely.

'Apparently she disappeared after visiting a hospital clinic?'

'Wrong.'

'Is it, sir?'

'Disappeared from the supermarket car park adjacent to Loston Hospital, actually, after leaving the clinic. We know she'd just been in the supermarket because she was caught on CCTV.'

'Wasn't there CCTV in the car park?'

'Normally there would have been. But a bloody bulldozer working on an extension to the supermarket dug up a cable and put the CCTV in the car park on the blink.'

'Hard luck, that.'

'These things happen, Speckle. Is that it, then?'

'Ah . . . no sir. What I really wanted to know is, which clinic at the hospital was she attending?'

'Isn't it in the file?'

'Sadly not, sir.'

'Bloody computers. Lost somewhere in cyberspace, no doubt. Nothing safer than a damn biro and a sheet of A4, I say. Oncology. Brain tumour. Good chance that she just wandered off, you know. Apparently she had been doing odd things. Well, it's what someone with a brain tumour does, isn't it – odd things.'

'That clears that up. Thank you. Just one other thing, sir. Two women who went missing at that time, Elinor Roebuck and Susan Finch—'

'Within days of each other, yes. What about them?'

'Do you know if they were friends or enemies?'

'Rivals. For the same man. You think that Finch murdered Roebuck, right?'

'The thought did come to mind, sir.'

'As it did back then, Speckle. But there was no proof.'

'Finch did disappear a couple of days after Roebuck went missing, sir.'

'Not proof though, is it? Anyway, back then Jack Allen, who led the Roebuck inquiry, and Harry Chalke, who led the search for Finch, left no stone unturned, I can tell you. And at that time the thinking was that one killer had likely done for both.'

'But it was a missing persons investigation, sir. Why would the police think murder so quickly?'

'About a month before two other women near Manchester had gone missing. Their bodies were found ten days before Roebuck and Finch went missing. Both had been raped. So it was perfectly understandable and reasonable to think that the same killer may have been at work again.' There was a brief silence on the line before Doyle said, 'He may still have been. Maybe he hid his third and fourth victims better than his first two, Speckle. And maybe he's hid a lot more, too.'

'If he raped his victims there must have been DNA?'

'Yes, there was. But the thing with DNA and all this scientific wizardry is that it isn't worth a pinch of snuff if it can't be matched up to someone already on the database. Then it's down to coppers to nab the bastard. Which, sadly, in this case they never did. Is that it, Speckle?'

'Yes. Thank you, sir.'

'Speckle!'

The DI was just about to replace the phone when Doyle's booming summons came down the line. Sally Speckle held the phone well away from her ear. 'Yes, sir.'

'This skeleton thing won't involve overtime, will it?'

'We're just at the initial stages of the inquiry. It's difficult to say, sir.'

'No, it isn't. Just say no! I daresay that there'll be more important things to do than finding out who these old bones belong to.'

'I'm sure the parents and relatives of the missing women wouldn't—'

The phone was slammed down.

'... See it that way, *sir*,' she added contemptuously.

'Sermon's having a twisted underpants day, isn't he?'

'That'll be Chief Superintendent Doyle, DC Rochester,' Speckle said. 'But, yes, he's having a twisted underpants day. When doesn't he have? And he probably hasn't seen this yet.' The DI took a copy of the *Loston Daily*, sister to the *Loston Echo*, from her desk drawer. The headline read:

WHO IS THE SKELETON IN THATCHER'S LOT?
POLICE BAFFLED.

'How could we be baffled? The skeleton was only found yesterday,' Speckle complained.

CHAPTER FOUR

The Roebuck house was, to the ordinary man, the stuff of dreams. A Tudor original. There were copies not so nearby because the Roebucks' gardens occupied at least three acres of Merry England to keep the neighbours at arm's length. The pretentious copies, built on acreage sold off by other houses (no doubt out of dire necessity), stood like expensive warts among the more traditional houses that were old England, as opposed to the newer en-suite private swimming pool and bar set that had cost an arm and a leg, but would always be the poor relation – plonk pretending to be vintage. When those in the quiet and reserved Tudor and Edwardian houses went to Barbados, they were following in the footsteps of those who had built an empire and never flew charter, and in other times would have taken a long cruise, every need catered for by a small army of servants.

DI Sally Speckle pressed the button on the intercom set

into the granite of one of the gate columns of Ivy Lodge.

'Yes?' The woman's voice was sharp, and created an image of country tweeds and afternoon tea.

'Police, madam,' announced Sally Speckle.

'Police?' the woman questioned annoyedly. 'What is it you want?'

'I think it would be preferable if we came inside, madam,' Speckle said.

'Do you indeed? Not a view I share! But we must not impede the constabulary in the pursuit of their duty, whatever that might be.'

The gates buzzed and swung open. Speckle looked appreciatively at the parked Bentley with a mere top-of-the-range Mercedes alongside it in the gravelled forecourt the length of an airport runway.

'Just as well you didn't drive the Punto into this lot,' Lukeson said.

'My Punto has served me well, considering the awful lack of care I've visited on it,' Speckle said.

A woman, presumably the woman to whom they had spoken, was coming from the house. She came to meet them, not out of courtesy, they reckoned, but rather to try and avoid lesser mortals entering the house.

'Mrs Roebuck?' Her lack of confirmation Speckle took as confirmation. 'I'm DI Sally Speckle. And this is DS Andy Lukeson.'

The woman looked at Speckle and Lukeson as if they were not far removed from what one was likely to find on one's shoe after a stroll across country fields.

'Well, then?' Emily Roebuck asked impatiently. But Speckle reckoned that Mrs Roebuck would be impatient most of the time.

'Emily . . .' A man came to the front door, beyond which was a hall that was long and wide enough to land a Boeing 747 on. He looked curiously at people who were obviously not the usual sort of visitor he might have expected to see. And then looked to the woman, presumably his wife, for an explanation.

'Police officers, Cyril,' she said curtly.

'Police officers?'

'Do try not to sound like an echo, Cyril,' she said. Andy Lukeson reckoned that Emily Roebuck would not suffer fools gladly. The direct-action type, he thought. 'What did you say your names were again?'

'DI Sally Speckle and DS—'

'Ah, yes. Lukeson. Knew a Simon Lukeson out in South Africa. That was before the government got the wind up and handed the place over to the er . . . *natives*.' Her face was proof positive that a picture spoke louder than a thousand words, only in Emily Roebuck's case make that a million words. 'Bloody idiots!' she added venomously.

Cyril Roebuck had the high colour of English country life, but the purple tinge of his lips indicated that his colour had more to do with blood pressure than the freshness of country living.

Andy Lukeson thought that runners rather than country squire brogues would be infinitely more suitable for the long journey to the front door.

'You ask them what they want, Cyril,' Emily Roebuck said. 'They won't tell me.'

Sally Speckle gritted her teeth.

'We've come about your daughter, Mrs Roebuck,' she stated in a clipped fashion.

'There must be some mistake, Inspector,' Emily Roebuck rattled off. 'We don't have a daughter.'

'Not now,' Cyril Roebuck hastened to explain. 'Elinor has been gone a long time, you see. Look, perhaps you'd better . . .' He stepped aside to let them enter, much to his wife's displeasure, who reminded her husband brusquely, 'Have you forgotten? We've a meeting of the Old Order Brotherhood to go to in a short while. And after that I've got the gym to go to.'

Gym. That explained Emily Roebuck's fitness.

'It's a kind of neighbour association,' Cyril Roebuck explained. He laughed. 'The Old Order Brotherhood, not the gym.'

'Neighbourhood association?' Emily Roebuck snorted. 'Good grief! It's nothing of the kind.' She went on to explain her version of the Old Order Brotherhood. 'It's a society that was set up a couple of years ago to keep England as it was intended to be. In fact, a more apt description would be *to restore England to what it once was.*'

Her face curled sourly.

'Civilized.'

Both Speckle and Lukeson were very well aware of the Old Order Brotherhood. Its doctrines and its sentiment had once been voiced before by a small, insignificant failed artist who had a flare for sporting a ridiculous moustache and spent his time, when he was not being thoroughly obnoxious and downright vile, flicking back his fringe from his forehead.

'Have you seen some of the monstrosities *they* call houses round here?' Emily Roebuck grimaced. 'Good God, I've seen better summer huts! And if we don't take a stand now we will be invaded by people whose birth should never have been permitted in the first place, and this country will become as grotty and as common as a caravan park.'

She looked to Speckle and Lukeson for sympathy. And got it from neither.

'Do you know that one day last week I heard from some garden or other a raucous sound, similar to the squealing of a stuffed pig, that was supposed to be music. And only the previous week—'

'Emily, dear . . .'

Emily Roebuck looked furiously at her husband. 'I'm sure whatever the content of your interruption, it is not of earth-shattering importance, Cyril. So please wait until I've finished before you speak.'

Speckle and Lukeson felt sorry for Roebuck. Andy Lukeson reckoned that the now rather diminutive figure had once been at least six feet tall, before being cut down to size so many times.

'Now, as I was saying—'

'I'm afraid we are rather pushed for time, Mrs Roebuck,' Lukeson interjected.

Emily Roebuck looked at Andy Lukeson with hostile contempt, obviously wishing that the failed artist with the ridiculous moustache was not around to ship him off in a cattle truck for extermination. On the other hand, judging by Cyril Roebuck's smug grin behind his wife's back, he was fighting an urge to slap him on the back.

'Please.'

Much to Emily Roebuck's displeasure, Cyril Roebuck led the way inside, ushering Speckle and Lukeson into a room to the immediate right of the front door. It would not do at all to have plodders reaching too far into the house.

'Aren't you joining us, Emily?' Roebuck asked, as his wife went upstairs.

'Why would I possibly want to do that, Cyril?' Her bemusement was genuine.

'The police are here about Elinor, dear.'

'Elinor left five years ago, Cyril.' She settled a steely gaze on Speckle and Lukeson. 'That was her choice. I say, so be it.'

'Left?' Sally Speckle questioned. 'You say that as if your daughter just decided to leave home?'

'What else?'

'Elinor was reported as a missing person, Mrs Roebuck.'

'Cyril thought it necessary, Inspector Sparkle.'

'Speckle.'

'Whatever.' Emily Roebuck settled her gaze on Sally Speckle. 'Elinor threatened many times when I tried to curb her rebelliousness that she woud leave home, and she did.'

'She was eighteen years old, Emily,' Cyril Roebuck said. 'Every teenager—'

'Should show respect, Cyril,' Emily Roebuck barked. 'Her father indulged our daughter shamelessly.' She scoffed. 'I'm afraid my husband, like all . . . *daddies*, can be quite the fool when it comes to their little girls, Inspector.' She fixed what Andy Lukeson would term a poisonous look on her husband. 'But if you took off the rose-tinted glass through which you looked at Elinor, Cyril, you would have seen that she was manipulative and cunning and quite the little schemer. And she was every bit as uncaring towards you as she was towards me, only you preferred to think of her as vivacious and high-spirited.'

'This is not the time to be discussing this, Emily,' Roebuck said firmly, straining at a leash that threatened to snap at any second. Speckle wondered what would happen if and when it finally did.

Emily Roebuck obviously thought about overruling her husband but, after seeing his already flushed face become more flushed still, she changed her mind. 'Will this take long?' she asked, reluctantly joining them.

'Not very long,' Andy Lukeson said, as diplomatically as he could, when he saw that Sally Speckle was also straining at the leash.

'You said it was about Elinor?' Cyril Roebuck said.

'Yes,' Speckle said. 'We're checking on women from around the time your daughter went missing, Mr Roebuck.'

'Why?'

DI Sally Speckle strained a little more on her leash at Emily Roebuck's demanding tone of voice. 'Remains have been found in Thatcher's Lot—'

'Oh, no,' Cyril Roebuck wailed.

'Do control yourself, Cyril.'

Speckle went on: 'The skeleton is that of a young female. It is early days yet and a great deal more analysis needs to be done, but a current estimation is that the skeleton has been in the ground for about five years.'

Cyril Roebuck was wringing his hands, and for the first time Emily Roebuck was shaken, the colour draining away from her face to leave a grey pallor that revealed the age hidden behind the careful and expensive make-up.

Cyril Roebuck staggered and slumped into an armchair, whimpering, leaving his wife to ask any questions that needed asking.

'And you think that these remains are Elinor's?'

'There is that possibility, Mrs Roebuck,' Speckle said. 'We're hoping that dental records will be of help in identifying the remains. If not, DNA will be needed. Who was your daughter's dentist, Mrs Roebuck?'

'It was Jack Armstrong,' Cyril Roebuck said. 'He has, or rather had, a practice on Grey's Quay. Retired now.'

'Do you happen to know where he has retired to, Mr Roebuck?' Lukeson enquired.

'Not very far, actually. He has a daughter over in Brigham with whom he's gone to stay. Until he becomes too difficult to manage, that is. Jack Armstrong has got Alzheimer's, I'm afraid. It's anyone's guess as to how quickly it will progress.'

'Do you know his daughter's address, sir?'

'Yes, Sergeant. It's 16 Arbour Square. Big Georgian monstrosity. Never liked Georgian myself.'

'How long before you can make an identification?' Emily Roebuck asked.

'Shouldn't take too long,' Speckle said. She addressed Cyril Roebuck. 'Did Mr Armstrong hand over to someone else?'

'Oh, yes,' Roebuck confirmed. 'Can't for the life of me just now recall his name.'

'Bernstein,' Emily Roebuck said. 'Jewish, you know. His first name was something biblical. But then all Jewish names are, aren't they?'

'Is Mr Bernstein being Jewish relevent, Mrs Roebuck?' Andy Lukeson questioned stiffly.

Emily Roebuck sniffed. 'I thought you police people would want to know every little detail of every little thing. Now' – she checked her watch – 'if that's all, Cyril and I do have that meeting of the Old Order Brotherhood to go to.'

'Not quite all,' Sally Speckle intoned.

'This whole thing is getting rather tiresome, Inspector Sparkle.'

The DI refused to rise to the bait by restating her name. What a bloody vicious bitch you are, Mrs Roebuck, she thought.

'Now about a DNA sample—'

'My husband and I really don't want to revisit that painful time, Inspector.'

'A DNA sample would prove beyond any doubt the identity of the remains. If it is Elinor, would you not want to bury her remains?'

'Why don't we discuss this matter again if and when you have determined that the remains are not those of another missing woman? Goodbye, Inspector.'

'And I thought dragons were extinct,' Andy Lukeson said, as the front door closed behind them. 'Pity that poor sod, having to live life under the same roof as her.'

'Cup of coffee before we head out to interview the Finches?' Speckle suggested. 'There's a coffee shop in that little square we passed through.'

'Why not? I need the caffeine.'

'I'd better get Charlie Johnson to go and see this Bernstein.' She phoned Johnson to pass on her instructions. 'Oh, shit,' she swore on hearing something Johnson had said. 'Bad? Yeah. OK. See you later.'

'What's happened?' Lukeson asked when she broke the connection.

'Helen Rochester walked into the door of an open locker and gashed herself just above the right eye. She's had to go to A&E. And that means we'll have to split up. Which do you fancy? Alfred Wright or the Finches?'

'I'll take Wright. I've had enough of the upper crust for one day.'

CHAPTER FIVE

DC Charlie Johnson tried everything to ignore the whirr of the dentist's drill, other than put a finger in his ears, which a young boy sitting alongside him had no inhibitions about doing. Others chose to flick through the pages of one of the well-thumbed out-of-date magazines common to doctors and dentists' waiting rooms, pretending that they were not at all bothered or anxious, but their nervousness was obvious from their flitting from one article to another. Charlie Johnson, working on the adage that if you can't beat them join them, flicked through the war in Iraq, the marital problems of a soap star, an article on country pastimes, and a diet which, if the success it claimed was even a tenth valid, DC Helen Rochester would lose the stone weight she had been trying to lose for as long as he had known her, starting each diet with new hope that was soon lost in swirls of cream which she seemed to have no resistance to. Just as he was becoming acclimatized to the whirr of the drill, it stopped and suction began. If there was one thing Bernstein's surgery needed it was better insulation. There was a couple of minutes' total silence before the door of the surgery opened and the unfortunate victim came out. He went to reception, where he made another appointment for the following week.

'Tuesday. Three fifteen OK?' the receptionist chirped cheerfully, the way a receptionist in a travel agent's might when you had finalized the details of a two-week vacation in some exotic location.

The man mumbled what must have been his acceptance, because the receptionist became even more cheery.

'Until Tuesday afternoon, then, Mr Cross.'

Defeated, Mr Cross left the waiting room.

The receptionist looked to Charlie Johnson. 'Mr Bernstein will see you now.' No cheeriness this time. Her tone of voice left him in no doubt that his interruption was unwelcome. 'As you can see, Mr Bernstein is rather busy,' she said, as she led him to a door behind reception which turned out to be the dentist's private office. 'Mr Bernstein will be with you shortly.'

The door closed, and as if one door was connected to the other, the other opened. Bernstein came through from the surgery, a waft of antiseptic in his wake. He went and sat behind his desk without uttering a word and looked curiously at Charlie Johnson before asking, 'In what way can I be of help, Officer.'

Bernstein completely ruined the stereotype image of what a Jew should look like. He was blond, almost Nordically so, had light blue eyes and smooth skin with (for those who can remember that far back) a Kirk Douglas dimple in a strong manly jaw.

'My grandfather fled Munich in '36,' Berstein said. 'Came to England and married an English Rose.' DC Johnson seldom blushed, but on this occasion he did. Bernstein had read his thoughts with unerring accuracy. He went on: 'My father, in turn, did the same, Officer. Hence, this very English-looking Jew.'

There was no rancour in his voice. In fact, he sounded rather amused.

'But, by the mysteries of genetics, I have a very Jewish-looking brother.'

DC Charlie Johnson introduced himself and thought about apologizing, but decided that there would be no point. Anything he said might only lead to further embarrassment. He could point out that in fact he was very tolerant and not in the least racist or anti-Semitic, but were he to do so, it would sound patronizing and would be as useful as spitting on a bushfire to quench it.

'I'm here about a patient of Mr Armstrong from

whom you—'

'Then why don't you ask Mr Armstrong about this patient?' Bernstein interjected pointedly, causing Johnson a needle of annoyance.

'Because,' he returned, even more pointedly (not off to a good start, he thought), 'you took over the practice from Armstrong, and presumably his patients, too.'

'Not all.'

'I have this list, Mr Bernstein.' Johnson placed the list of missing women on Bernstein's desk. 'Perhaps if you'd just look through it and tell me if—'

'None,' he said perfunctorily, after a glance.

'Might I suggest a closer inspection, sir.'

'No need, Constable.'

'Most of them would probably not be patients of yours' Charlie Johnson let his eyes wander meaningfully round the plush office. 'But there is one name at least, Elinor Roebuck who was a patient of Mr Armstrong's, and possibly another also – Susan Finch.'

'Like I've already said, Constable. None of the names on your list is familiar. If, as you say, Elinor Roebuck was a definite patient of Mr Armstrong's, then all I can say is that when Mr Armstrong sold the practice to me, she must have moved to another dentist. May I ask why you're enquiring?'

'The remains of a young woman were found in Thatcher's Lot. A preliminary estimate is that the remains have been buried for about five years. All of the women on that list went missing around that time.'

'And you were hoping to identify this woman by her dental records, presumably?'

'Yes, sir.'

Bernstein stood up. 'Sorry I can't be of more help.'

Johnson produced a copy of a file picture of Elinor Roebuck. 'If you'd just take a glance at this, sir.'

'I'm rather busy, Constable,' Bernstein complained.

DC Charlie Johnson shoved the photograph of Elinor Roebuck at him.

'No, sorry,' he said curtly.

'Well, that seems to be that.'

'Afraid so. Now I really must get back to my patients.'

'Presumably Mr Armstrong left you his patients' files?'

'Yes. That would be necessary to continue the treatment of any patient who chose to become my patient.'

'Nothing that might have been missed? You know, a couple of files stuck in a drawer somewhere.'

'Certainly not! Patients details are on computer now.'

'Mr Armstrong was an elderly gentleman. He might not have been into computers. Perhaps your receptionist might know if—'

'Sarah came with the new fittings and me, Constable.'

'And Mr Armstrong's secretary?'

'Retired with him, I dare say. She was not a young woman. Aged along with Armstrong.'

'Would you have her name, sir?'

'Frances. That's all I know.'

'So you wouldn't have Frances's address, then?'

Bernstein shook his head. 'Is that it?' he asked impatiently.

'I expect so, sir. Thank you.'

The surgery door closed on Bernstein. Charlie Johnson let himself out of the office. Crossing the waiting room and seeing an elderly woman, he decided to play a long shot. He sat down in a vacant seat alongside the woman. 'Pardon my boldness, madam,' he said. The woman looked at him with no small amount of apprehension. Charlie Johnson thought it was time to produce his warrant card. 'May I ask if you were a patient of Mr Amrstrong?'

'Yes. Almost since the day he opened for business. Why?'

'And, of course, you knew Frances?'

'Frances?' she asked vaguely.

'Mr Armstrong's receptionist.'

She gave a little shy laugh. 'Oh, you mean Franny! Lord, she hated being called Frances, you know.' Johnson could not imagine why. Franny was bloody awful. 'Yes, of course I knew her. In fact we became quite close friends.'

She looked at Johnson with a touch of alarm.

'The police. Has Franny gone and done something daft?'

'Oh, not at all,' Charlie Johnson quickly reassured the elderly woman. 'Quite the contrary. We think that Franny might be able to help us with our enquiries.'

'Really! That will perk her up no end, I'm sure.' She leaned close to Johnson and he got a whiff of brandy. Who could blame her, facing Bernstein's chamber of horrors? 'Between you and me, Franny always liked to be the centre of attention.' She rolled expressive eyes. 'Full of her own importance she'll be now. I dare say that it would be best not to visit her for a day or two.'

'Visit her?'

'Yes. Oh, of course, you couldn't know, could you? Franny took a bit of a tumble. Resting up in Loston Hospice after coming out of hospital. Fit as the proverbial fiddle, is Franny. Be out and mucking around in her garden in no time at all. Indestructible is Franny Clements.'

The elderly woman leaned close to Charlie Johnson again.

'What kind of enquiry would that be?' she asked.

Charlie Johnson side-stepped the question. 'Mrs Gerrard is the matron of Loston Hospice, isn't she?' He knew she was because in the Pick Up case, Loston Hospice had featured prominently.

'Pain in the arse! Runs the place like Dachau.'

'You've been most helpful, Mrs—'

'Miss Benton,' she interjected. 'Lotty Benton. Franny and I both had the hots for the same man, you know.

Then he went and married an American from Idaho.' She made 'American' sound like something to be despised, second only to Idaho. 'So Franny and me had spent so much time chasing Charles Watson that when he upped and left for America, every other eligible man had taken a wife and we were on the proverbial shelf and quite out of date.'

'How unfortunate.'

She chuckled bronchially. 'How bloody lucky, you mean. Charlie Watson was arrested for defrauding the bank he worked for and had to go on the run. In South America, I believe. Can't see Franny or me on the run with him, can you?'

'Never,' Johnson said. He took Elinor Roebuck's picture from his pocket, 'Lotty? I may call you Lotty? Did you ever see this young woman here in the surgery?'

Lotty Benton studied the photograph of Elinor Roebuck, and decided: 'Yes. I have seen her here. When she was all gawky and awkward. About sixteen then, I would say.'

Charlie Johnson's brief moment of elation vanished.

'But not later when Mr Bernstein took over the practice?'

'In the surgery, you mean?'

'Yes.'

Lotty Benton shook her head. Charlie Johnson sighed. It had been worth a try.

'But I did see her in Mr Bernstein's company. Of course,

that would be about five years ago now. They were dining in that new posh restaurant that opened about then.' She shook her head as if trying to shake the ellusive name of the restaurant from her subconscious. 'Fan ... Fan ... something or other.'

'Fandangos?' Charlie Johnson prompted.

'That's it. Quite expensive, I believe. Way beyond my pocket, I'm afraid,' she confided. 'I was passing when I saw them, just inside the window.'

'How did they appear?'

'Appear?'

'Were they friendly?'

'Well, he wouldn't have taken her to dinner if they weren't, now would he?'

'Business, perhaps?'

'What kind of business would a girl, little more than a child, have with Mr Bernstein?' That's what DC Charlie Johnson was thinking. 'Cosy,' Lotty Benton said, considering the word for a moment before repeating, 'Yes, I'd say they were cosy. Quite cosy, in fact.'

DC Charlie Johnson eased himself off the chair alongside Lotty Benton and thought about going back to challenge Bernstein, but decided that strategy should take precedence over impulsiveness. He went to leave, feeling quite chuffed that his initiative had paid off so handsomely.

'You never told me *your* name,' Lotty Benton said.

'Charlie.'

'Yes, yes. You look like a Charlie,' Lotty Benton said, quite unaware that she might have given offence.

'People sometimes say that, Lotty,' he chuckled.

'Oh, good grief,' Lotty wailed. 'I didn't mean—'

'Of course you didn't. Bye.' Charlie Johnson closed the door gently behind him.

CHAPTER SIX

DS Andy Lukeson turned into Buxton Street and his spirits immediately plummeted. Buxton Street was a long, narrow, dreary parade of old fifties council houses that, had anyone had the mind to, or decency, should have been flattened long ago.

The street was dominated by an old mill, long since defunct and ever more rapidly falling apart, its entrances boarded up and covered with weeds. The mills had ceased production in the late sixties when textiles from Asia began to flood the market, providing cheap throw-away clothing that they were not equipped to compete with, due to years of trade-union restrictive practices and demarcations, and no small measure of management by class rather than by experience. A man might carry the oil can but he could not pour the oil. And the manager who missed lunch at one o'clock on the dot was considered to have been guilty of bad form. Nothing like that in Asia, the very bedrock of multi-skilling where working days ran one into the other in non-stop production seven days a week and for wages that any swag from Bowles would have spent just tasting the ale in the local pub.

The soot from the two chimney stacks had eaten into the brick of the houses, turning what was once bright red brick to a dirty yellow with just the odd streak of defiant red running through it. So intense had the soot been that the joinings between the bricks had disappeared completely, covered by a black crust of soot and dust that on a hot day still seeped.

It surprised Lukeson that some developer had not moved in to demolish the mill and put in its place a shiny new apartment block, but his surprise was short-lived. Who, in their right mind, would want to look out on Buxton Street? Perhaps if the streets behind Buxton Street did not repeat the same soul-destroying drabness there might have been some hope of renewal. But with government budgets getting tighter every year, Lukeson reckoned that it would be the lot of Buxton Street to fall apart house by house until all that was left was rubble for the developers to remove before they began redevelopment.

A football flashed past Lukeson's face and smacked off the wall of the old mill. A group of young tearaways on the opposite side of the street sniggered.

'Oi, Benny,' said one of the boys who came forward with the swagger of a natural leader, 'where's your manners? You nearly gave the old geezer a heart attack.'

Those behind the leader huddled together in even greater merriment.

'That weren't nice,' another boy said, timidly. 'Sorry, mister.'

The leader glared at the boy who had spoken. 'You do as we do, Lenny Bains. Or you're out.' Now Lenny's apology was to the leader, who did not accept it graciously. 'I think you're a bit poncy anyway to be hangin' round wiv us.'

The boys walked away, encircling their leader and excluding Lenny from their number. Lenny hurried after them, pathetically trying to become part of the group. But as they turned the corner at the end of Buxton Street, despite his best efforts, Lenny remained an outcast. Andy Lukeson wondered for how long the boy could suffer exclusion before he forfeited his decency as the price of inclusion, and Buxton Street would produce another criminal or depressed down-and-out.

Number twenty-one was midway along the street and, if possible, even brought down the tone of Buxton Street. The small garden was littered with rubbish. Greasy takeaway wrapping and rusting beer cans. A bicycle frame without wheels was its centrepiece, like a nonsensical piece of modern sculpture. Ship it off to one of those trendy new galleries and it would probably fetch a fortune from a twat who had more money than sense, Andy Lukeson thought. The entire place was littered with pigeon droppings, with any free space taken by stray dogs. Lukeson stepped over the rotten wooden gate which no one had bothered to pick up. It had lain there for a long time, judging by the old dirt clogged underneath it. An usptairs window was broken and an orange curtain with white stripes blew in the breeze without any great enthusiasm, like the flag of a country that was ashamed of its existence.

Lukeson tried the bell but, like the rest of the house, it had long since stopped functioning, so he hammered on the door knocker. Specks of what had at one time been red paint but had now become colourless fell like dandruff from a combed head. He was about to knock again when the door was yanked open by a beer-bellied man in vest and underpants who seemed ready to punch the lights out of whoever had disturbed him. He smelled of stale body sweat, stale onion, and equally stale beer.

'What d'ya want?' he barked.

'Alfred Wright?' Andy Lukeson enquired.

The man was instantly suspicious. 'Who wants to know?'

DC Andy Lukeson flashed his warrant card.

'Must be gettin' old,' Wright said. 'I'd have recognized a copper in a sniff before.' He laughed, if the throaty growl could be described as such. 'At least you ain't a bill collector.' He scratched his groin, not in the least embarrassed to show his testicles. Then he transferred the half-eaten sandwich in his left hand to his right hand with which he had scratched himself, and repeated the process with his left hand on the opposite side of his groin. Lukeson came to the conclusion that in Alfred Wright he was sure that he had found the missing link, and wished he had not. 'Want to come in, I suppose. Coppers always do.'

He turned and walked back along the hall, which was almost a replica of the garden. That he could see, the wheelless bicycle frame and pigeon droppings were the only difference. Wright had to step over two stinking dogs of indeterminate breed to reach the room he turned into. Not a lover or a truster of canines since, as a young boy, he had been bitten, Lukeson would have preferred not to have to step over the dogs, but as it turned out they were much too lazy to work up the energy to bite.

The room into which he followed Wright had at some time been a sitting-room which had been converted to a tip. The 3.15 from Plumpton was just starting, and that at the moment was the centre of Alfred Wright's world and his sole reason for living.

'No guff 'til this is over,' Wright ordered.

The race was only a couple of minutes long. In fact, for those who had not betted on Dandy Boy, the runaway winner who, judging by the expletive-fluent Wright, was obviously not among their number, the race was over in the first twenty seconds. Dandy Boy built up a lead from the rest of the field that widened over the length of the race until Dandy Boy flashed past the post with Country

Breeze, Dandy Boy's nearest challenger, completely out of shot.

'Why can't we breed nags like the bleedin' Irish can?' Wright grumbled. The betting docket he had torn up and thrown in the air descended on Lukeson like a snow flurry. 'OK.' He threw himself on to a sofa which once had a red rose pattern, its lustre long since buried under grease and grime. 'You've got ten minutes before the 3.30.'

'I've come about your niece Linda, Mr Wright.'

'Alf. That's what me friends call me.' Andy Lukeson reckoned that Wright would not name him among his friends, and Lukeson would not want him to. He also thought that Wright's circle of friends would be a pretty small but not very select group. 'Dead, ain't she, our Linnie? That's what we called her – Linnie.'

'Dead?'

'Yeah. Dead.'

'How can you be so sure?'

Of course he could be, Lukeson thought. If Alfred Wright had murdered her. In police parlance, Wright was *known to them*. He had a temper. A couple of times he had escaped jail by the skin of his teeth for being involved in bust-ups, mostly in pubs. And would have gone to prison for putting his wife in hospital after a fierce beating if she had not lost her courage and withdrawn the charges.

'It's been five years since Linnie disappeared. And you lot didn't get near findin' her neither. She'd have come home if she weren't dead.'

'Well, we may have found her now, Wright,' Lukeson said.

'Yeah?' Wright said, hiding his dark secret, if he had one, behind a blank stare.

'The remains of a young woman was found buried in Thatch—'

'Read about that.'

'The remains were in the ground for about five years—'

'That's about the time Linnie disappeared.'

'And therefore we are checking on women who went missing round that time.'

'Many, were there? Went missing, I mean?'

'Can we stick with Linda,' Andy Lukeson said tautly.

'Could be Linnie, I suppose. She was on the game. Meet all sorts on the game, don't ya?' He groaned. 'Never wanted nothin' to do with her. Knew she'd be trouble like her mum before her. "You're her uncle, Alf", me wife said. "The kid's your responsibility. It'll be nice havin' a kid round", she said. She couldn't have none,' he added bitterly. 'Then, when Linnie was eight years old and startin' to get into trouble, Annie – my wife, the tramp – ups and takes off with a bloke who came to fit new windows, leavin' me with Linnie. Mightn't be able to have kids, but she could open her legs sure enough! For a fuckin' window fitter!'

Andy Lukeson reckoned that on a social scale of ten, a

window fitter would be way ahead of Alf Wright.

'If Linda was getting into trouble, why wasn't she put into care?'

'Never did nothin' about it, that's why. It weren't serious trouble then. But when she was thirteen she met an older bloke who got her started on heroin, and then used her to feed his own habit by arrangin' for men to come to his gaff; blokes who fancied kids, because that's all Linnie really was. She was fifteen when he overdosed. I begged her to come home, but by then she was a street slag, out of her skull most of the time, chasing the next fix.'

'On the night she disappeared, you were with her.'

'What's that supposed to mean?' Wright hotly challenged Lukeson.

'It's in the statement of a witness who was in the same pub as you and Linda. This man would have reason to remember. You threatened him with a broken glass.'

'When I went to the loo, he tried it on with Linnie, didn't he? What would you do? Ask him to pray with you, eh?'

'As I said, you were with Linnie. You argued with her. Threatened to wring her neck, the barman said. Linda stormed off and you followed her.'

'To reason wiv her. But when I got outside, she was at the end of the street gettin' into a big posh car. That's in my statement to you lot. Not that it did any good. You never found the car, did ya?'

'There wasn't much to go on. A big car doesn't say

much. You couldn't tell the investigating officers the make or colour of the car.'

'I said I thought it was black.'

'Do you know how many big black cars there are, Mr Wright? And what if it wasn't black to start with? I'm sure the investigating officers did—'

'Nothin'!' Wright barked. 'Linnie was from a place like this. People from Buxton Street don't matter much to coppers. And she was a junkie on the game who had gotten into a posh car. You lot didn't give a toss, did ya?'

Aware of how cases were prioritized, DS Andy Lukeson knew that Alf Wright's charge held more than a grain of truth. A perusal of the files of the missing women showed a lot more activity in the search for Elinor Roebuck and Susan Finch, who hailed from addresses that were light years away from Buxton Street; addresses in which the residents knew where and how to apply the pressure, pressure that filtered down to senior officers who in turn, with the odd exception, yielded.

'You didn't go back into the pub that night?'

'I was skint.'

'Did you come directly home?'

'The coppers already asked me all of this. You thinkin' like them, eh? You thinkin' that I topped Linnie, is that it?'

'Did you, Mr Wright? Kill your niece?'

Alf Wright studied Andy Lukeson. 'At least you have the balls to come right out wiv it, that I grant ya. Them other coppers was right pussy-footers. I'll tell you like I told them. I went for a walk.'

'Did anyone see you?'

'No. It was a real quiet night.'

'How long did you walk for?'

'Fifteen, twenty minutes maybe. To clear me head.'

'That's a long time to walk without being seen or seeing anyone.'

Alf Wright shrugged.

'Had Linda a dentist?' Lukeson asked quietly.

'A dentist?' Alf Wright snorted. 'She was a pros with a mouthful of teeth rotten by heroin. What do you think, copper?'

'Then to make a positive identification we'll need a DNA sample. Would you be willing to give one, Mr Wright?'

'Yeah. I would. But wouldn't her sister be a better match?'

'Linda had a sister?'

'Yeah. Her mum, me sister, had two kids. Linnie was the second, come two years after Laura.'

'Where can I contact Laura?'

Alf Wright hunched his shoulders. 'Moves round a lot. Last I heard she was shacked up with an Irish bloke over in Brigham. Flaherty, I think his name was. Used to drink at the King's Head, a couple of streets over. The barman's been there since the flood. He might know exactly where Flaherty is now. Irish, too. They stick together, that lot, don't they?'

'Thanks for your help, Mr Wright,' Lukeson said.

As Andy Lukeson left, the horses were lining up for the start of the 3.30 at Plumpton, but Alf Wright seemed to have lost all interest. It was, he thought, rather ironic that the favourite's name should be 'Cards on the Table'. Presumably the horse's owner was, like him, an Agatha Christie fan.

'Hey!' Andy Lukeson paused on hearing Wright's summons. He beckoned him back to the front door. 'Before I say anythin', you heard nothin' from me, understood?'

'Agreed, Mr Wright.'

Alf Wright looked around before he spoke again, and when he did it was in a whisper. 'You might want to talk to a bloke called Pearly Stevens. He's called that cos he spends a fortune keepin' them gleamin'.'

Lukeson had heard of Stevens, as every copper in Loston and further afield had. However, after several years of trying to build a case that would put George 'Pearly' Stevens away for the very long time he deserved, they were no nearer achieving their goal. Pearly Stevens was both a very clever and a very careful man. He had the knack of always being somewhere very public when his thugs were carrying out his orders. And his rise to prominence in the criminal world had been spectacular.

'He used to deal in Thatcher's Lot, before he got too big for his boots. Linnie used to get her stuff from him there, she told me. O' course, now he's got an army of thugs to do his dirty work for him. Used to own the Blue Stocking club before they tore it down and built apartments on it. Pearly lives in the penthouse.' Wright shook his head vehemently. 'Told Linnie that upsetting Stevens was stupid. Poisonous bastard that he is.'

'Upset? How?'

'I don't know. Linnie just told me that she did.'

'When was this?'

'Coupla weeks before she disappeared.'

Most of the information which Alf Wright had passed to him was old news, except the bit about Linda Wright getting her drugs from Stevens in Thatcher's Lot. Maybe whatever angst there was between Linda Wright and Stevens came to a head in Thatcher's Lot?

'I didn't say nothin'. Right?'

'Not a word, Mr Wright.'

The door closed in Lukeson's face.

As he reached the end of Buxton Street, he saw the boy called Lenny sitting on an upturned rubbish bin, head bowed. Obviously he had not been allowed to rejoin the group of young tearaways. Another time he might have talked to him. But nowadays older men approaching children was not something that was done.

Andy Lukeson was glad to leave Buxton Street behind.

CHAPTER SEVEN

Melissa Scott had risen late and she would swear that the cornflakes (her normal breakfast fare) she was eating tasted different at midday than they did at seven in the morning. But it was probably the flu she was at home from work with rather than anything different about the cornflakes. She pushed the bowl away and picked up the newspaper her husband Simon had left on the kitchen table before he had gone to work that morning. There was a note under it that read: 'Go and see the doctor, Melissa'. At first reading, one might be of the mistaken assumption that her husband's concern was solely for her. However, Melissa knew better: they were going on holiday to France at the weekend and Simon did not want to be inconvenienced. Inconvenience was something that angered him, one of the many things that sent him into a rage these days. He seemed forever on edge. The newspaper was the previous evening's edition of the *Loston*

Echo, but though it was old news, to her it was current.

SKELETON FOUND IN THATCHER'S LOT GRAVE BURIED FOR FIVE YEARS.

The headline screamed out at Melissa Scott, bringing back a rush of memories from the vault of her subconscious where they had been stored when no answers could be found to them five years previously. She read on, jumping ahead to take in the full story as quickly as she could. And as she read, every detail of that day in Thatcher's Lot five years previously came vividly to life, as if she were right there. She could even smell the July vegetation of the Lot. Feel its spongy softness underfoot. The drip of rain after the light shower from which she had taken shelter under a tree while she had waited for Elinor Roebuck to turn up.

Other images crowded in, too. Music. Big band music. The kind of music that had been playing in the Blue Stocking club on its wartime night, six years ago. A nostalgic trip down memory lane.

'The White Cliffs Of Dover' was being sung when Elinor had come in that night. So vivid were the pictures flooding out of her subconscious that now Melissa Scott almost repeated the wave she had given Elinor Roebuck that night when she came into the club. She could see Elinor's flashing smile of recognition and her squeezing through the crowd.

'Jam-packed, isn't it?' she had said, as she sat at the

table Melissa was sitting at, along with her then boyfriend Frank Boyd, and another girl who was anxiously checking the entrance when she was not checking her watch.

She could hear Elinor's voice as if she were there in the kitchen with her.

'This is Frank,' Melissa had said, introducing her boyfriend. 'Elinor.'

Elinor and Frank had shaken hands very formally. She had waved to David Dees (the Blue Stocking's resident DJ, comedian and drag artist) at the other side of the club. Elinor had turned round to see who she had waved to. Dees, who had been heading for the dressing-room entrance near the stage, changed course and came to their table. Elinor knew of David Dees, but had never actually met him.

'This is my night for introductions,' Melissa had laughed. 'David Dees meet Elinor Roebuck.'

'I just have time for a dance,' Dees said, and swept Elinor on to the dance floor. When they arrived back at the end of the dance, Melissa could see that Elinor was smitten. 'We'll dance again later,' David had said, no doubt in his mind that his invitation would be accepted. 'After I've done my Miss Tarty-Tawdrey bit.'

Miss Tarty-Tawdrey was the name David Dees took for his risqué drag act, depicting a lady of the manor who had a voracious appetite for a bit of rough. And as always, it brought the house down.

'Will you just look at that fabulous shoulder-bag with

those great big brassy strap rings,' Elinor had said. She had laughed then. 'I wonder what my mum would think if I got one just like it? Probably choke.' Her green eyes lit up. 'Maybe I could borrow David's.'

Melissa Scott recalled that when David Dees had come off stage, an ugly scene had developed between him and a girl called Susan Finch, a regular at the club, and one of Dees' many conquests. Only Susan had not understood the rules of the game and had sought exclusive rights, which David had rejected.

'Who's that?' Elinor Roebuck had asked.

'Her name is Susan Finch. And you'd better watch your back. Susan has it bad and she has a temper.'

As promised, David Dees had returned to dance again with Elinor; a dance that Susan Finch had watched venomously from the edge of the dance floor.

Melissa Scott set the *Loston Echo* aside, troubled. She wondered if she should contact the police. Tell them about the meeting with Elinor in Thatcher's Lot (Elinor had phoned in a right tizzy) to which she had not turned up. She had been interviewed when Elinor had gone missing, but she had not mentioned the meeting, supposing that Elinor had gone off some place to think and she would turn up when good and ready. And when, after several weeks Elinor had not done so, she felt that mentioning the meeting then would have her in all sorts of trouble with the police.

She had stood under a tree from a shower, and that's

when she had seen the man with the metal detector. She had placed no importance on it back then, but now that remains had been found in Thatcher's Lot, she was seeing this man in a more sinister way. She would probably phone the police later. But there was someone else she needed to phone first. Fortunately, she still had the phone number after all this time.

CHAPTER EIGHT

Dr Blackman inserted the last of four stitches in the gash over DC Helen Rochester's right eye and stood back to examine his surgery. 'You'll be as good as new in a couple of days,' he promised. 'There might be a small scar, but that will fade away in time. Meantime, it will probably scare off the Saturday night yobbos. And if you'll just come back, say, Thursday, we'll have a look.' He grinned with boyish charm. 'And try not to walk into any more lockers. OK?'

'He fancies the pants off you, me thinks,' the attending A & E nurse whispered to Rochester.

Get away,' Rochester laughed. 'He's just a nice man.'

But, Helen thought, if he does fancy me, I'll have a bit of that. His six feet and one or two inches perfectly matched her five foot eight, and he had a very good body. Pity she was in a steady relationship with a bloke from Traffic. Otherwise, she'd be up and panting.

Blackman turned from writing up his notes. 'You might have a bit of a headache. Nothing that a couple of paracetamol won't cure.'

'Thanks for everything,' Rochester said.

His boyish grin was hack.

'My pleasure entirely, Helen,' he said, turning back to complete his notes.

'There you are,' the nurse said. 'He's terrible with first names, but he remembered yours.'

'Have you got someone to see you home?' Blackman enquired, but this time continuing to write up his notes.

'I think he's gone off me,' Helen said, tongue in cheek. 'Yes, a colleague came along with me who'll see me home.'

'A female colleague?' Blackman enquired casually.

'Male.'

Was it her imagination, or had Blackman shown a glimpse of displeasure at the news? 'Lucky chap, your colleague,' he said affably. Yes, it was her imagination. 'Escort Helen to whoever is waiting for her, Nurse Crawford.'

A flatteringly anxious PC Brian Scuttle stood up in the waiting room on seeing Rochester. 'Bloody hell, I thought they were doing a heart transplant.'

'Nice to see you too,' Helen said with a cheeky grin. 'Thanks, I'll be fine now,' she told the nurse. She shook off Scuttle's hand on her arm. 'I'm not your granny, Brian!'

'How many stitches?'

'Four.'

'Ten grand a stitch, makes forty thousand.' Helen Rochester glared at her partner. 'OK. Only joking.' They walked along for a couple of paces, then: 'Twenty a stitch, I reckon.'

They were at the door of A&E when Nurse Crawford caught them up. 'Can I have a word?' she asked hesitantly, as if she regretted the request as soon as she had voiced it.

'Of course,' Rochester said.

'It's about the skeleton that was found in Thatcher's Lot. Do you know who it is?'

'Not yet. Takes time.' Helen Rochester studied the nurse. 'Do you think you know who it might be?'

'A woman by the name of Christine Walsh, maybe. She went missing about five years ago—'

'Yes. Christine is on our list of missing women from around that time,' Rochester said with interest. The nurse went on in a rush, as most people do when facing the police: 'The newspapers say the skeleton has been in the ground for that time. Christine disappeared in the supermarket car park after leaving the oncology clinic here five years ago.

'I was a junior in the clinic. A dogsbody. I got to know Christine rather well. We weren't friends as such. Just chatting in the clinic. At the time she was the only young person attending. The rest were from middle age upwards, so we formed a kind of natural alliance, I suppose.'

Nurse Crawford's face took on a new degree of worry. 'In a way, I blame myself for what happened.'

'Why is that?'

'Christine would get a cup of tea after she'd finished her treatment; everyone does. A cup of tea and a biscuit. Standard tea and standard biscuit. One day, Christine said, "Do they get these by the lorry load?" The biscuits are very plain. So I had a packet of figrolls in my locker and I went and got them. "My favourites", Christine said.

'Blackman – he was at the clinic then, too – came into the rest room, "Mine too", and joined us.

'"Had the measles once", Christine told us. "My mum got me figrolls every day as a treat, and I became a figroll junkie". Anyway, I mentioned that the supermarket had figrolls at half price. And that's why Christine was at the supermarket the day she disappeared, you see.'

'It was not your fault that Christine disappeared,' Rochester said reassuringly. 'She disappeared because some evil bastard took her.'

'But if I hadn't mentioned that the supermarket had half price fi—'

'You have nothing to worry about,' Rochester repeated. 'Sorry, I've forgotten your name.'

'Crawford.'

'Well, Nurse Crawford. Like I said, you have nothing to worry about. Yours was an act of kindness to a sick person.'

'Never thought of it like that.'

'Well, that's the way to think about it,' Helen Rochester said, squeezing the nurse's hand.

'You two had something in common, you know. Christine was the only other person – woman – whose name Blackman remembered. I think he fancied her, too.'

'Oh, why did you have to go and tell me that?' Helen wailed theatrically. 'Now you've spoiled everything.'

Crawford had a moment's concern, before she saw the smile on Helen Rochester's face.

'For a copper,' she laughed, 'You're quite the piss-taker, aren't you?' Nurse Crawford was alerted by Rochester's glance beyond her. Blackman had come to the surgery door and he was looking at them, somewhat annoyed, Rochester thought. 'Got to run.'

Helen Rochester patted the dressing over her right eye. 'See you on Thursday, then.'

'Off, I'm afraid.'

'Well, another time then, perhaps?'

'Yeah. Maybe we could go for a drink sometime?'

'Why not? We can talk about the kind of anuses men are.'

'Good idea,' PC Brian Scuttle piped up. 'It's a really interesting pastime. We do it all the time about you lot.'

Crawford laughed and hurried back along the hall.

'Home?' Scuttle asked.

'Don't be daft. Back to the station.'

'You're not even going to take a sickie?'

'No. I'm perfectly fine.'

'You're a traitor to the working class, you are.'

Getting into the car, Rochester paused and looked across the hospital car park to the adjacent supermarket. 'Wonder if there's anyone working there now who worked there when Christine Walsh went missing?'

CHAPTER NINE

The supermarket manager's name tag said 'Robert'.

'I doubt it,' he said, in reply to the question that had exercised DC Helen Rochester ten minutes before. 'People move round all the time. It's really hard to get staff to stay for very long. Spend a fortune training them, and as soon as they know their way round they up and leave,' he complained.

'Were you here then?' Brian Scuttle enquired.

Robert looked at Scuttle as if he had taken complete leave of his senses. 'No,' was his blunt answer. 'I'm only here six months.'

'Train someplace else, did you?'

'Yes. But they were absolute shits to work for. So I moved on right after training.'

Scuttle exchanged an amused glance with Rochester.

'It's different for managers,' Robert said, interpreting the exchange of looks perfectly. 'Anyway,' he said, pouting, 'as I was saying, staff seldom stay that long in any one place.'

As far as Robert was concerned, the interview was over.

He pouted even more when Helen Rochester said, 'We'd appreciate if you checked . . . Robert.'

'I'm very busy,' he retorted petulantly.

'Aren't we all, my son,' PC Brian Scuttle said.

Hating to have to yield ground, Robert called a passing member of staff. 'She'll know if anyone does,' he said disparagingly. 'Here since the bloody flood. The exception that proves the rule, you might say. No one else would probably have her in the way.'

When the middle-aged woman arrived, Robert's smile was beatific. What a shit he truly is, Rochester thought.

'Sheila, I want to pick your brains,' Robert gushed. 'You were here five years ago, right?'

'Yes,' Sheila confirmed. 'Been here seven years, actually, Mr Cornton.'

It was ridiculous, Helen thought. A woman in her fifties calling a man young enough to be her son mister.

'Yes,' Cornton said wearily. 'But it's only five years ago that concerns the police.'

Sheila looked nervous. 'Don't know if I know anything that the police will want to know, Mr Cornton,' she said defensively.

'That remains to be seen. So' – he waved a hand at Rochester and Scuttle – 'over to you.'

Robert Cornton hurried away, berating another woman

about not having reduced the price of waffles.

'Hello, Sheila,' Rochester said, in what Andy Lukeson called her come hither voice. 'I'm DC Helen Rochester and my colleague is PC Brian Scuttle.'

'What did Mr Cornton mean by helping you?' Sheila asked. Looking like a trapped animal, she backed away as far as the shelving behind her would permit.

'It's nothing to worry about,' DC Rochester reassured the woman. 'It's just that you were working here five years ago when a woman disappeared from the car park—'

'Awful, that. Yes, I remember.'

'On duty that day, were you?'

'Yes,' Sheila said, relaxing. 'Terrible, it was. Did the police ever find her?'

'I'm afraid not, Sheila.'

'Oh, dear. Must be a gonner, then.'

'We're still hopeful,' Brian Scuttle said.

'After all this time? That's a bit optimistic, isn't it? Downright silly, if you ask me. Thought you lot could have done more, meself.'

Sheila had really come out of her shell.

'About that day,' Helen Rochester said, getting the conversation back on track. 'Did you see Christine Walsh?'

'Was that her name?'

'Yes.'

'I'd forgotten,' Sheila said, a little guiltily. 'Poor thing.'

'Did you see her?' Rochester was trying valiantly to contain her exasperation. Brian Scuttle was close to losing his composure, Sheila's criticism not having gone well with him.

'Yes.' She pointed. 'Right over there.' Helen Rochester turned round to look at where Sheila was pointing. It was the music section. 'I passed by quite close. She was looking at an Abba CD. I was surprised. I thought she'd be more into that awful heavy rock or dance music. Abba were very musical, you see.'

Sheila frowned.

'There was a bloke watching her.'

'There was a man watching her?'

'A man's a bloke, ain't he?'

'Right. Yes, of course. What kind of man, Sheila? Tall? Small? Thin? Fat?'

'Tall. About six feet, maybe a little more. Thin, but not skinny, if you know what I mean.'

'Muscular build?'

'Yeah. That would describe him all right. Really fit, I'd say. Took care of himself, that one.'

'Can you describe him?'

'No.'

'But he was quite close by, you said.'

'Yeah. He was. But it was raining that day. He was wearing an anorak, with the hood up. Not supposed to do that in a supermarket, I think. Have the hood up. Or is that in a bank? Anyway, didn't see his face.'

'Did he follow Christine outside?' Rochester pressed.

'Dunno, do I? I had me work to do.'

'And you didn't see Christine in the car park?'

'I did. I was on the deli counter that day. Back then it was by the window over there, looking out on the car park. I turned round to take some chickens that were ready out of the oven and I saw her crossing the car park. She went between the cars, on the blind side of a van, one of those high-sided vans, and that was the last I saw of her. I told the police all this already,' Sheila complained. 'Don't you write everything down?'

'Yes, we do. Just checking.'

'She left the car park real quick.'

'What do you mean, left the car park real quick?'

'Well, when I turned back to put a tray of sausages in the oven, she was gone.'

'How long was that?'

'Seconds. Come to think of it now, she could have hardly made it from behind the van in that time, let alone leave the car park.'

Robert Cornton breezed back.

'Finished, are we?' he intoned sarcastically.

'I best get back to work now,' Sheila said.

'Just before you go, Sheila. Can you recall if there was a name on the van? The name of a company, maybe?'

Sheila screwed up her eyes, and after due thought said, 'No. No company name. It was just a plain white van.'

'Was there a car parked alongside the van, blindside?'

'Yes.'

'Can you recall the make of car?'

'No. Just saw the back, really. Nothing much more than the tail lights.'

'Colour?' Rochester enquired hopefully.

'Grey,' Sheila stated instantly.

'Dark? Light grey?'

'What my Arthur calls a metallic grey. I suppose more silver than grey in a way. My Arthur had one the same colour around that time.'

'Might it be the same model, then?'

'I suppose.'

'And what model did your Arthur drive, around that time?'

'Oh, you've got me there, love. But I can ask him.'

'Great. You can contact me at Loston CID. Ask for Helen Ro—'

'Oh, no need for that. Arthur's the maintenance man here.' She went to an extension phone on a nearby desk and punched two digits. 'Arthur, love, remember the make of the car you drove about five years ago? Yeah, the grey one. Thanks, love.'

She replaced the phone.

'A Mondeo.'

'Thank you, Sheila,' Helen Rochester called after her, fleeing the aisles under Robert Cornton's glare.

On leaving the supermarket there was a sign that read in big bold letters: FIGROLLS HALF PRICE.

'Wouldn't all of this have been caught on CCTV? Brian Scuttle said. He looked around him. 'Must be more cameras here than Fort Knox.'

'All pointing to see across the car park.'

'That's my point,' Scuttle said.

'But it didn't matter on the day Christine Walsh vanished. The car park CCTV wasn't working on that day. A bulldozer had dug up the cable.'

'Maybe whoever grabbed Christine knew that,' Scuttle speculated.

'Maybe they did at that,' Rochester agreed. 'But I'm sure that the investigating officer had everyone who might be privy to that information in for questioning. It would have to be someone working in the supermarket or at least close to it to have known that a bulldozer had knocked out the CCTV. But—' Helen Rochester stepped into the car park and looked back to where Sheila had said that the deli was situated at the time Christine Walsh went missing, and then looked out over the car park. 'Do you know what I think happened, Brian? Sheila saw Christine go behind the high-sided white van, and when she looked back seconds later she was gone, having left the car park, Sheila thought. However, she hadn't. I think Christine Walsh was kidnapped or got in voluntarily to the car on the blindside of the high-sided van.'

PC Brian Scuttle looked with admiration at Helen Rochester. 'That's bloody clever,' he complimented.

'But, five years on, also bloody useless!'

'Not really. We'll have a starting point if the remains found in Thatcher's Lot turn out to be those of Christine Walsh,' PC Brian Scuttle said.

Getting into the car, Rochester said, 'Christine wasn't grabbed. That would have created a fuss. She got into the car voluntarily. As soon as I get a chance, I'm going to start checking on grey Mondeos around the time Christine vanished. You never know what might pop up, eh?'

CHAPTER TEN

Speckle thought on entering the village: Close your eyes and think Miss Marple. It was a twenties picture postcard, and Speckle reckoned that it must have taken enormous effort to stay the march of progress that had befallen a great many English villages, much to everyone's shame; that they should have so glibly destroyed a unique heritage by allowing estates that could no longer be afforded and farms that had become unviable to have fallen into the dreaded developers' hands to end up as cramped estates of matchbox houses with a proliferation of wheelie bins, unkempt greens dotted with saplings that would never grow into fine oaks and beeches that were uprooted to get in another couple of matchboxes, another cul de sac or another so-called avenue.

The village was dominated by a Palladian mansion that shouted: Hands off, I'm here to stay. From a stroller, Speckle learned that the Finch residence was at the far side of the village. The elderly man pointed with a walking stick, as if the house was nearer to Land's End than just at the other end of the main street, as it turned out. The house stood proud and majestic in ivy-clad magnificence. And this house had an avenue that merited the dictionary definition: an avenue that ended in a circular gravelled forecourt surrounded by meticulously manicured lawns, flower beds, rockeries and shrubs with, of course, the obligatory oaks and beeches and other great trees. Not a weed dared to raise its scruffy head.

A maid opened the front door, and DI Sally Speckle could only think that she had come on the butler's day off.

'I'm here to see Mrs Finch,' Speckle said, showing the maid her warrant card.

'I'll tell her you're here, madam,' the maid said. 'If you'll just step into the morning-room.' The maid showed her to a room just to the right of the front door. The maid left, closing the door softly behind her.

Looking around her at the magnificently proportioned room, Sally murmured, 'I'll never be able to afford this on a copper's pension.'

A couple of minutes and the door opened again, every bit as softly, and Mrs Finch entered, paused just inside the room and haughtily studied her guest. Sally Speckle had a feeling of being in a play, Finch's entrance had been so well stage-managed – a murder mystery, of course.

'Mrs Finch?'

Mrs Finch did not confirm her identity, but asked, 'Why are you here?'

'I'm DI Sally—'

'Same name as my maid,' Finch interjected.

—Speckle.'

'English, is it? Speckle?'

'Yes. But would it matter if it weren't, Mrs Finch?'

It would not surprise Speckle if, like Emily Roebuck, Finch was a fully paid-up card holder in the Old Order Brotherhood.

'What is it you want, Inspector?' Finch enquired brusquely, obviously not used to the brazenness of the cheeky underclass. Sally Speckle consoled herself with the thought that one day Old Hollow might be a mess of sapling dotted greens and wheelie bins.

'I've come about Susan's disappearance five years ago, Mrs Finch.'

Finch's reaction knocked the DI back.

'How tiresome.'

'Tiresome?'

'Digging up the past.' She produced a parody of a smile. 'If you'll pardon the pun, Inspector, it's a useless exercise.' Her pause was so perfect that Speckle wondered if Finch had been an actress who had snared a squire. 'You see, Susan was not my daughter,' she explained. 'Something' – she glanced to the ceiling and beyond – 'that I shall be eternally grateful for.'

She elaborated: 'I married Phillip, Susan's father, four

years ago. And last year I became widowed when Phillip, who had this ridiculous idea that he was twenty years younger than he was, died in a jet-skiing accident in the Canaries.'

And I bet you did not shed any tears, Speckle thought.

'So, you can understand why' – she said "you can understand", in a manner that indicated that Speckle was one of the underclass's brighter ones – 'I am not animated by either Susan's discovery or her fate, Inspector.'

Mrs Finch fixed Sally Speckle with what could be justifiably described as a *beady* eye.

'I take it that the skeleton found in Thatcher's Lot is Susan?'

'No positive identification has yet been possible, Mrs Finch.'

'Then why—'

'Am I here? To try and make that positive identification, of course. Has Susan a sibling?'

'A brother. Dubai. At least that's where Andrew was the last I heard. Likes dead things. He's an archaeologist,' she explained. 'Why would you want to know where he is?'

'If we can't make an identification by other means, such as dental records, we may need to take a DNA sample.'

'Thank heavens I'm useless for that.'

Sally Speckle charitably supressed the thought that Mrs Finch was pretty useless for anything other than prancing about as the lady of the manor. However, her charity was not wholly successful.

'Did you get on with Susan?' Speckle asked, pretty sure of what the answer would be before it was given.

'We had our disagreements, Inspector.'

She had been right.

'Disagreements or outright arguments, Mrs Finch?'

Finch was offended that one of the underclass should so brazenly pressure her. 'Like I said—'

'I know what you said, Mrs Finch. I'm simply trying to establish the degree of your *disagreement*. Might Susan have disapproved of your marriage to her father?'

'Might I suggest that you're stepping outside your brief, Inspector!'

'My brief, Mrs Finch, is to identify the remains found in Thatcher's Lot and bring to justice the person who murdered Susan – if the remains are those of Susan – and buried her,' the DI stated emphatically.

'Would you like some tea?' Mrs Finch enquired.

'No thanks.'

'Then I shall.'

She went to a bell pull. Sally Speckle was astonished that something as Victorian as a bell pull should exist in a house that had probably been built after the heyday of master and servant. A different maid to the one who had admitted her appeared with unnerving silence, to ask with a french accent, 'Can I be of service, madame?'

'Yes, Mimi. Tea.'

'Yes, madame.'

'For two, should the inspector change her mind once

she smells cook's home-made biscuits.'

'Madame.'

The French maid glided soundlessly out of the room. Speckle wondered if there was some school or academy that trained servants to glide.

'Please.' Mrs Finch indicated that Sally Speckle should sit in the twin of the armchair she was occupying. 'Susan was a silly, brazen, out-of-control little slut,' she stated.

'That, to me, sounds a lot more than a little spat, Mrs Finch,' the DI said.

'Not only did she disapprove of my marrying Phillip, she actually found Phillip and I in bed which, considering her liberated spirit, she took grave exception to and went on to make life hell for me.' She gave a little bitter laugh. 'A classic case of the kettle calling the pot black, Inspector.'

'I take it that Susan's reason for her great distress was that at that time you were Phillip Finch's mistress?'

'How very astute you are.'

'Did Susan tell her mother?'

'Oh, no. She was much too clever to throw away such a pearl of blackmail, Inspector.'

'Blackmail? Susan blackmailed you?'

'And her dear papa. But she wasn't interested in money. No, the price for her silence was that Phillip should turn a blind eye to the rather unsavoury company she kept.'

'And he agreed?'

'It was that or a very expensive divorce.'

'I thought his worry might be that his wife might find out.'

'His wife find out?' She laughed. 'Phillip didn't care a fig about hurting Isabella. His only concern was the preservation of his wealth. And, truthfully, that was my only concern also,' she added with blunt honesty.

Mimi came back and placed a silver tray of tea things on the table. 'Shall I pour, madame?'

'No.' Finch waved her away.

The French maid glided ghostlike out of the room again.

'Will you...?' Finch waved a hand over the silver teapot.

Sally Speckle did not change her mind. She would prefer to have tea with Hannibal Lecter.

'So, it would be fair to say that with Susan... *out of the way*, life for Susan's father and you was less fraught?'

'Very fair to say, Inspector. But, if by *out of the way* you mean, did I off the silly little bitch, the answer is no. And before you ask, neither did Phillip. Even though he had a daughter from hell, he worshipped the ground Susan walked on. Which, frankly, made me thankful that Phillip did not make me pregnant. I should hate to think that any act of mine would perpetuate the Finch rottenness and idiocy.'

She poured her tea and looked across the teapot at Sally Speckle.

'I suppose you're shocked by my bluntness, Inspector?'

'It's not very often we come across such forthrightness, Mrs Finch.'

'I seduced, bedded and married Phillip Finch for his money and' – her hand waved about – 'all of this. Mercenary, of course, but I'm not the first and indeed I shan't be the last to grasp the chance of a lifetime.

'And Phillip was no innocent. He took, very liberally, of what I offered and hadn't a care for who was hurt. He intended, of course, to divorce Isabella. But there was the problem of a considerable slice of his fortune going with her. Did you know his wife Isabella had committed suicide shortly after Susan disappeared?'

'Threw herself in front of an underground train on a visit to London. Northern line, I believe. The stupid woman doted on her brat of a daughter. Got into a terrible state when Susan vanished. Isabella became convinced that she had been murdered, and that it was all her fault. Such a silly woman.'

DI Sally Speckle had a very dark thought. What if the present Mrs Finch (to circumvent the divorce issue) had gambled on Isabella's reaction to Susan's disappearance, and had murdered Susan Finch in the hope of precipitating that reaction? Clearing the way to marry Phillip Finch, fortune in tact. She had to be at least twenty-five to thirty years Phillip Finch's junior. A short wait and the Finch millions would fall into her lap.

'Do you know Susan's movements on the day she disappeared, Mrs Finch?'

'Only as relayed by Phillip through pillow talk. It seems she had the most awful row with Isabella and stormed out of the house in a fury. Foolishly upset, Isabella followed her to try and reason with Susan.'

'Followed her to where, do you know?'

'I don't. Phillip never said. The night he told me all of this was his birthday and I was ... well, you might say, giving him his birthday present, Inspector. Sure you won't change your mind and have tea? These biscuits are quite delicious.'

Speckle ignored the invitation.

'Have you any ideas about where Susan might have gone, Mrs Finch?'

She shrugged disinterestedly. 'Perhaps to the Bernstein house.'

Sally Speckle perked up. 'The Bernstein house?'

'Yes.'

'He's a dentist, right?'

'Yes, again.'

'Was he Susan's dentist?'

'Yes, Inspector. I'm impressed.'

Melissa Scott hurried to answer the knock on the door of her flat. On opening the door, she said, 'I'm so glad you came. I was going to phone the police, but I thought it would be better if we talked first. Please, come in.'

Melissa Scott wondered what the sharp pain in her chest was. But she did not have long to wonder. She was dead in seconds.

CHAPTER ELEVEN

DC Charlie Johnson was on his way back to the station when his mobile rang. He pulled over to answer, because he had a thing about drivers who used mobile phones while driving. Observing the habits of other drivers, he sometimes wondered if he was the only one with such a concern. Spotting a vacant parking space, he cut sharply towards it. The car behind him honked furiously. Looking in the mirror, Johnson held up a hand in apology, only to see the angry driver on a mobile phone. 'Bloody cheek!' the DC shouted as the motorist swerved round him and shot past. 'Hello,' he bellowed into the mobile.

'Shit, Charlie,' Sally Speckle grumbled. 'Why bother with a phone at all? Just stick your head out the window.'

'Sorry,' he said grudgingly, his anger at the driver still bubbling. 'Traffic should do something about drivers using mobile phones,' he complained, his frustration making him oblivious, until it was too late, to the sound of a moving car coming over the mobile.

'Too tight, are they?' Speckle asked.

'What?'

'Your underpants, Charlie. Now, listen.'

'I'm listening.'

'Have you seen Bernstein?'

'Yeah. On my way back to the station from talking to him. Why?'

'Bernstein lives in the same village as the Finches.'

'Interesting, that, boss.'

Speckle gave Johnson the gist of her interview with Mrs Finch, finishing: 'She thinks Susan might have gone to Bemstein's house after a bust-up with her mother on the day she went missing. And Bernstein was her dentist.'

'He's a lying git, boss! I asked the bastard about Finch and he said he didn't know her. But then, he also said that he didn't know Elinor Roebuck. But Lotty says she saw him having dinner with Elinor in Fandangos restaurant.'

'Lotty?'

'It's a long story.'

'It'll keep, Charlie. Did you confront Bernstein with this information?'

'No. I thought I'd run it by you first, boss.'

'Thanks, Charlie. I appreciate that.'

Sally Speckle took Johnson's consideration as a positive sign that she was being seen by the trads as being worthy to be numbered among their ranks.

'Get back to Bernstein, Charlie,' Speckle instructed.

'Right away, boss.'

*

Bernstein's nervous fingers tapped on his desktop. 'It was stupid of me, Officer, to deny knowing Susan Finch.'

'Yes, it was,' Johnson said, stony-faced.

'It was just an impulsive thing. A spur-of-the-moment reaction. Sorry.'

'So.' Charlie Johnson's face became even stonier. 'Why don't you fill me in, Mr Bernstein. Truthfully this time.'

'Of course.' Bernstein swallowed hard and wiped away the sheen of perspiration on his forehead. 'The afternoon of the night Susan Finch disappeared she came round to my house in a pretty dreadful state. Apparently she had had the most fearful row with Isabella, Susan's mother,' he clarified. 'Turning up on my doorstep the way she did put me in quite a spot, me being a friend of her father's and a regular visitor to the house.'

He wiped away more perspiration from his forehead.

'Phillip had confided in me that Susan had taken up with a rather unsavoury bunch and had become quite argumentative and rebellious. It seems that this all started after Susan became a frequent visitor to a club of the day called the Blue Stocking.

'Phillip told me that the club was owned by a very repulsive sort called Pearly Stevens.' He laughed nervously. 'So named because of his pride in keeping his teeth whiter than white. A patient of Armstrong's, I believe. Anyway, my first reaction was to drive Susan home . . .'

'Why did she come to you in the first place?' Johnson questioned.

'I presumed because of my friendship with her parents, Officer.'

'And your friendship with Susan Finch? Was that a close friendship, sir?'

'Oh, no. Not at all.'

DC Charlie Johnson did not believe him. His denial had been much too quick and too vigorous, he thought. 'Please go on, Mr Bernstein.'

'Ah, as I was saying, my first reaction was to drive Susan back home. But events overtook me, I'm afraid.'

'In what way?'

'I glimpsed Isabella approaching through some trees that were on a rough patch of ground near my house. The site of a demolished house that was never rebuilt. I mentioned to Susan that her mother was coming and, before I could stop her, she ran into the house.

'I immediately asked her to come back and talk to Isabella. She refused point blank and ran upstairs into one of the bedrooms and called down that she was undressing and that if I let her mother in she would say that we were lovers.

'Susan quickly amended that to say that she would tell Isabella that I had tried to rape her. She was out of her mind, Constable. A madness no doubt induced by whatever illegal substance she had taken. Phillip had mentioned that he had found cocaine in her bedroom.

'I was beside myself. I shut the door and pretended not to be home when Isabella called. Luckily for me, Rachel, my wife, had gone into Loston.'

'Luckily, sir?' Johnson intoned. 'Hardly. If your wife had been at home you wouldn't have found yourself in such a pickle.'

'Yes. I see your point.'

'So, what then?' Johnson enquired.

'Isabella finally got tired of leaning on the bell and left.'

'Did Susan Finch leave also?'

'Yes, she did.'

'Soon after, sir?'

'About half an hour later.'

'Slow dresser, was she?' Johnson asked.

'What are you implying?' Bernstein protested.

'When did your wife get back?'

'She didn't, actually. Get back, I mean. She stayed late in Loston to see a play at the Kimber Theatre.'

'On her own?'

'Yes. I get claustrophobic in cinemas and theatres. I was once in a cinema that burned down, you see. And since then, frankly, being in any theatre or cinema scares me witless.'

'What time did your wife come home?'

'Late. Very late. Early hours of the morning, in fact.' Charlie Johnson remained silent and let the silence do his work for him, compelling Bernstein to explain, 'It's not what you think.'

Samuel Bernstein shifted uneasily in his plush chair.

'Absolute frankness is needed at this point,' Johnson said, implying by his tone of voice that were the dentist to be less than truthful on this occasion, things would not go well for him. 'Obstructing the police in an investigation is a serious matter,' he added, by way of a further incentive for Bernstein to be frank.

'I can depend absolutely on your confidence, can I, Officer?'

'Goes without saying, sir.'

'My wife goes to Loston once a month to meet her illegitimate son. It was a mistake a long time ago, when Rachel was very inexperienced and very young. Ben, her son, turned up out of the clear blue one day last autumn, and she was rather captivated by him. You see, Ben was the only child Rachel could ever have. So, the third Saturday in every month, when Ben gets an afternoon off from the fast-food place he works in, they meet.'

'Always the same Saturday?'

'Yes. Like I said, the third Saturday of every month.'

'Susan Finch went missing on a Saturday, sir. The date, the twenty-second, would suggest that it was the third Saturday of the month. It's easily checked.'

'Good God! Do you think Susan. . . ?' Bernstein was a good actor – a very good actor indeed in Charlie Johnson's opinion.

'Think what, sir?'

'Well, picked that Saturday to call?'

'Is that what you think?'

'If she didn't, it was rather a coincidence. Susan must have known that I'd be alone.'

'Would your wife not have been sympathetic to Ms Finch, sir?'

'No. She thought Susan was a spoiled brat.'

'What did you think. Of Susan, I mean?'

'I thought Susan wasn't all that bad, really. She was nineteen years old. Didn't we all kick up a fuss when we were that age? But Rachel adored Isabella Finch. Thought she was an absolute saint to put up with her lot. They have a son, of course. More of his mother's genes than his father's apparently. But he's out in Dubai, messing about in ruins. Archaeologist, you know. Came home reasonably often when Isabella was alive. Left immediately after her funeral and hasn't been home since. Skipped Phillip Finch's funeral. Can't say that I blame him for not wanting to come home and face that awful woman Phillip married after Isabella died.'

'Your wife—'

'What about her?' Bernstein interjected curtly.

'She wouldn't be pleased, Susan turning up on the doostep when you were alone in the house, would she, sir?'

'I think we'd better get off the track you've got on to, Constable,' he snapped. 'Rachel trusts me completely.'

Foolish woman, Johnson thought.

Bernstein's receptionist popped her head round the

door. 'A bit of a delay building up, Mr Bernstein.'

'Won't be long,' Charlie Johnson informed her.

'There's nothing more I can tell you,' Bernstein said.

'Did you tell Susan Finch about your wife's regular Saturday visit to Loston? Because, you see, if she called to your house specifically, she must have known that you'd be alone. Because by your own admission, your wife had little time for Susan Finch. So she would be unlikely to call if she were home.'

This time Bernstein's hand was wholly inadequate to wipe the sweat from his brow – a bath towel would have been needed.

DC Charlie Johnson said, 'Again, you're not being entirely frank, are you, Mr Bernstein?'

The dentist's shoulders slumped in defeat.

'It was a silly sort of thing,' be blurted out. 'A barbecue at the Finches. I had a little too much to drink, and somehow I ended up in the folly with Susan. It wasn't even sex in a serious way. Just a lot of fumbling and kissing. It might have been more, but Phillip Finch had his own plans for the folly that night. Susan and I barely got out in time.

'After that Susan became mischievous. I had to play along. Rachel would have kicked me out, and Phillip Finch would have skinned me alive.'

'Were you the reason for the argument between Isabella Finch and Susan, sir?'

'No. Something silly like Susan wanting to bring some

DJ from the Blue Stocking club to dinner. My understanding was that the Finches would not have had him in the doghouse.'

'Did Susan Finch say where she was going when she left you?'

'She was meeting someone.'

'Did she say who?'

'No. But I expect it was this DJ. We had had an argument about her seeing him. She was quite excited about this meeting, because of some rivalry for this man between herself and another woman.'

'Do you know who this other woman was?'

'A woman by the name of Elinor Roebuck, I believe.'

'Was it an intense rivalry?'

'Susan said that if Elinor did not bow out, she'd ... *do* her. But at the time she was in a tantrum and I'm sure that she didn't mean *do her* in the common meaning of the term.'

'Susan Finch went missing a couple of days after Elinor Roebuck did,' Johnson pointed out.

'You aren't seriously suggesting that Susan harmed Elinor Roebuck, are you?'

'There was that threat, sir.'

'I told you. Susan was in a—'

'Tantrum. I know. But maybe her anger lasted longer than anyone knew. And finally, Mr Bernstein, we believe that Susan Finch was a patient of yours?'

'Yes. And like I say, it was stupid of me to lie. But I

thought that I'd be drawn into a police inquiry.'

'You have been,' Johnson stated flatly. 'A bit unethical, wasn't it? Being the lover of one of your patients.'

Bernstein blanched.

'Was there a dental record for Susan Finch on file?'

'Yes, there was. But when Susan went missing . . . well, I destroyed it.'

'Why?'

'Panic. I had been having an affair with Susan. I anticipated that sooner or later, if Susan had been the victim of foul play, that she would be found and this would happen. So I didn't want to leave in place the most nebulous connection to her.'

'You were taking a chance on your receptionist not saying something.'

'She wasn't involved. I did what needed to be done myself.'

'Would it be fair to suggest, sir, that judging by your actions you seemed pretty certain that Susan Finch would not be . . . returning?'

'Susan was running with a wild crowd. Doing drugs. That she might have been the victim of foul play was, I suggest, a reasonable assumption.'

'Where were you the night Susan Finch went missing, Mr Bernstein?'

'That was five years ago.'

'But a day surely that stands out in your mind. Not easily forgotten, those kind of days.'

'I was at home. Alone. Well, until the small hours when Rachel got back.'

'Did your wife say where she'd been?'

'She said she went to a play she wanted to see in the Kimber Theatre.'

The Kimber Theatre was on Grey's Quay. In fact, directly across from the Blue Stocking Club. Might Rachel Bernstein have known about Susan Finch and her husband? Might she have seen Finch coming or going from the Blue Stocking Club (it was a Saturday night and the odds on Finch being at the club were good), confronted her, argued, lost the plot and killed her? Or perhaps Rachel Bernstein was more organized and waited for Susan with every intention of killing her in cold blood?

'If you don't mind my saying so, sir, you don't sound entirely convinced that your wife was where she said she was. Would that be right?'

'Rachel and I don't live in each other's pockets, Constable. Is that it?'

'Not quite, sir. Elinor Roebuck.'

'We've been through all this,' Bernstein responded narkily.

'Fandangos, sir?'

Bernstein held his head in his hands. 'It isn't what it seems.'

'I'd love to hear what it is, then, sir.'

'I met Elinor Roebuck with Susan Finch one day. I

jokingly said that we might have dinner one evening. And the next thing I know is that Elinor is waiting outside the door at the end of surgery to hold me to it. And I thought it would be easier to simply have dinner to avoid embarrassment.'

'And after dinner, Mr Bernstein?'

'I went home.'

'Pity Ms Roebuck can't verify that, eh? Isn't it, sir?'

CHAPTER TWELVE

Alec Balson said, 'Knife. Under the ribs and up into the heart with considerable force. Hardly any blood. Dead in the blink of an eye. The incision was narrow at the point of entry but got wider as the blade went in, which means that it was a knife with a blade that got wider along its length and' – he lifted the edge of the wound – 'the blade had a serated edge.'

Balson beckoned.

'See here.' Speckle and Lukeson bent to have a closer look. Speckle surprised herself that she was not now as squeamish as she had been on her first case when there was blood and gore aplenty. How quickly one can become desensitized, she thought. 'Those little sawtooth marks at the lower edge of the wound. A good guess would be that the murder weapon is a kitchen knife.'

Balson frowned thoughtfully.

'Another good guess would be that you're looking for

a bread knife, possibly.'

Andy Lukeson looked at the zig-zag pattern of what little blood the heart pumped in the second before it had stopped beating, and it suggested that the woman staggered back from the door and fell just inside it where a small pool of blood had gathered. Which meant that Melissa Scott could have been stabbed when she opened the door to her killer. He had already checked the kitchen knives and they were all present and correct. They had bagged the knives, of course, for analysis. But to the naked eye they looked perfectly clean. It would appear that Melissa Scott's killer had come prepared to kill. Lukeson shared his thoughts with both Balson and Speckle and they agreed with him that what he thought had happened had been the way Scott had met her death.

'We could do without this right now, Andy,' Sally Speckle complained.

Two DIs in Loston CID were out on sick and compassionate leave, one with an asthmatic attack, the second recovering from the death of his daughter in a car accident, and a third who was within days of retirement, so Doyle had reckoned that assigning him to the murder would be pointless because in a couple of days a new DI would have to take over and Doyle feared that in the changeover something vital might be missed which could end in having an unsolved murder on Loston CID's books. And to add to their woes the retiree's vacancy had not been filled, the result of yet another pruning of costs exercise. There was lots of talk about new technology having to be used to the full. But no one (and the people who knew better, and who could influence decisions remained silent) seemed to realize that, though technology had its advantages, that when it came to catching criminals a copper (the human variety and not the plug-in model) was needed to nail them. Machines were fine. But nothing yet had matched the intricate thought patterns of the human brain. When the machines reached that stage, humans would likely end up with two choices – clear off to some other less advanced planet or surrender to the nearest euthanasia centre.

'Shelve this skeleton business until the dust settles, Speckle,' Doyle had ordered.

'We've been making good progress, sir,' she had protested.

'She's waited in the ground for five years – what's the hurry? It won't do any harm if she waits a little longer, Inspector.'

Sally Speckle bravely risked getting 'Sermon' Doyle's dander up more than it already was. 'But she, whoever she is, was also murdered, sir.'

'But not hours ago, Speckle! It's a matter of prioritizing.' Budgetspeak for lack of adequate resources to get the job done. 'Anyway, what are the real chances of finding this woman's killer, five years on?'

'Only last week, sir, Thames Valley solved a twenty-year-old murder.'

Doyle glared at Sally Speckle. 'Thames Valley and what they get up to is none of our concern, Inspector. But the affairs of Loston CID are.'

'I think the team could run both investigations in tandem, sir.'

The chief super, though uneasy with the proposition, gave it some thought and concluded: 'Without incurring extra expense, like budget-sucking overtime?'

'They are a dedicated lot, sir.'

With a great heave of his massive shoulders, Doyle agreed, but he added a rider: 'The skeleton business is the minor part of this arrangement. Understood, Speckle?'

'Understood, sir.'

And as she was leaving: 'No overtime, remember!'

'Sir,' she intoned, closing the office door quietly.

'Was that wise?' DS Andy Lukeson asked a couple of minutes later when she told him of the deal she had struck with CS Doyle. 'We're stretched as it is, Sally.'

She had been a touch disappointed at Lukeson's criticism. She had come to expect (and had got) his wholerhearted support. But perhaps that had been out of kindness during the Pick Up case, it being her first murder investigation. After due consideration (once her initial disappointment subsided) she could understand his concern; a concern he now voiced in no uncertain manner.

'We can't keep going all the hours God gave us, Sally.'

'You're right, of course, Andy,' she conceded. 'It's just that I hate to put something I'm committed to on the back burner. I'll go and tell the chief super that we can't manage both so we'll shelve the skeleton case.'

She was heading upstairs when Andy Lukeson said, 'Wait. Look, the team will have to do most of this extra work. So why don't we put it to them?'

Sally Speckle pretended to give her sergeant's suggestion deep thought, but she was bluffing. The enthusiasm for his proposal was bubbling inside her.

'It's an idea, Andy,' she said, neutrally objective.

He laughed.

'What?'

'If you ever quit being a copper, I reckon you'd make a hell of an actress or poker player,' he said.

'I don't know what you mean,' she protested, uselessly.

Andy Lukeson had once more showed his ability to read people like an open book, irrespective of how opposite a pose they struck to their true feelings.

'Come on, then,' he said, walking off ahead of her. 'Let's put it to a vote.'

A short time later, all the facts having been placed before them, particularly the one about no extra overtime, the team's decision to keep both investigations running was unanimous. DC Charlie Johnson, always the joker, picked up the phone on his desk.

'I'd better tell those four women I'm currently satisfying that there's not enough room under my desk to continue making them delirious.'

'I don't think regulations would allow it anyway,

Charlie,' Helen Rochester said.

'Neither would the chief super,' WPC Anne Fenning piped up. 'It would take weeks of extra overtime to satisfy one. I don't think we'd have enough money in the kitty for four.'

'Not going to find much here, I reckon.' Speckle's reverie was interrupted by the senior officer of the forensic team. 'I'm guessing that the killer never stepped beyond the door of the flat.' Conscious of the importance of forensic evidence in catching a killer, and to convince a jury who had become used to the idea of forensics ('the telly-copper generation' Lukeson had called them) as being the yardstick for a conviction, the absence of forensics would be a great drawback. In the main, juries were no longer prepared to give too much weight to an investigating officer's opinion, and Speckle understood their reluctance to do so after several high-profile miscarriages of justice. 'Might be something on the landing or the stairs. We can hope. Pity it's not one of those modern apartment blocks, all marble and steel. Makes it easier to spot things.'

He glanced out the door of the flat.

'That old stairs carpet will be a nightmare.'

'Ready to go,' Alec Balson said, having prepared Melissa Scott's body for removal, careful to preserve any trace evidence there might be by placing plastic bags over the head, hands and feet. 'And before you ask,' he said to Speckle, 'I'll get a prelim report to you ASAP.' Now he indulged in the same complaint he indulged in at their previous meeting and every crime scene Balson had attended at. 'I wish they'd make these things (these things being the white overall worn at a crime scene) in a size somewhere between leprechaun and clown. And preferably to fit an ageing police surgeon whose earlier fondness for sugar and spice and all things gooey has come home to roost.'

'Her sister found her, right?' Speckle asked the young PC who had been first on the scene in response to Liv (short for Olivia) Benson's 999 call.

'Yes, ma'am.'

'Where is she now?'

'A neighbour across the hall took her in for a cuppa. Shall I fetch her, ma'am?'

'Better not. We'll go to her. All this will just upset her more than she already has been.'

'Not a pretty sight, ma'am,' said the young PC, with what she suspected would be his ruddy complexion, based on his ginger hair, still pale.

DC Helen Rochester and PC Brian Scuttle were obviously as welcome at George 'Pearly' Stevens' door as a bad smell in a perfumery. Stevens, being a man who could sniff out a copper from a mile away, would have had no difficulty at all, even if Scuttle were in civvies, in determining the profession of his visitors. He did not wait for the customary request for entrance. He simply stepped aside.

'Nice,' Rochester commented on the opulence into which they entered. 'Breaking bones and feeding drugs to youngsters pays handsomely indeed.'

'Now if I was a mean-minded man, I'd be on the phone to my solicitor right now,' Pearly Stevens said. 'Seeking damages for defamation.'

'The truth is not defamatory,' Rochester said.

Stevens smirked. 'Being a truthful man, I agree. This' – he waved his hands about – 'is all through my ceaselessly hard and honest efforts to improve my lot. And that makes your remarks on its legitimacy very hurtful.'

'Give over, Stevens,' Scuttle barked. 'Your kind gives scum a bad name.'

'And you'd be?' Stevens enquired of Rochester. 'Just for the record, should a record be required.'

'I'm DC Helen Rochester and my partner is PC Brian Scuttle.'

Pearly Stevens settled a leery gaze on Rochester. 'Into every day a little sunshine comes, eh, Detective Constable?'

'Enough of the niceties,' Rochester said. 'Let's get down to business, shall we?'

'And what business would that be?' Stevens asked, his mask of congeniality of a few seconds before vanishing behind a scowl.

'As the former owner of the Blue Stocking Club—'

'Ah,' Stevens sighed. 'The good old days, eh? Ever been, Constable?' he enquired.

'I prefer to avoid sewers,' Rochester quipped.

'Really? Then why did you become a copper? Filth, they call you lot, isn't it?'

'Keep this up and those pearly whites you spend a fortune on will be down your throat!' Scuttle barked, edging threateningly towards Stevens.

'Defamation and threat,' Stevens crooned. 'My solicitor will have a field day.'

DC Helen Rochester was angry with Scuttle. His tendency to react to goading, which every copper has his or her share of, was a flaw she wished he would work on controlling, if not overcoming completely.

'Let's get back to the Blue Stocking and its activities,' Rochester said.

'And what activities would they be?' Stevens enquired mildly. 'The Blue Stocking is a long time ago, and as I get older I find that my memory is not as good as it used to be, Constable Rochester.'

'We all know that the Blue Stocking was a conduit for your drug dealing and other criminal activities,' Scuttle growled.

'You know, Detective Constable,' Stevens sneered. 'I'm beginning to think that the coffers of the Loston Constabulary will not be sufficient to right the wrongs done me. It's really shameful that a *business* man of my standing has to suffer these scurrilous allegations.'

Helen Rochester shot Brian Scuttle a *watch it* look, just as he was about to wind up for what she expected was a go at Pearly Stevens.

'Now' – Stevens checked his gold watch – 'if you could get to the point, Constable Rochester. I'm expecting guests shortly and I wouldn't want any bad odours to spoil their visit.'

The temptation to take the leash off Brian Scuttle was an overpowering force which Helen Rochester had to muster every ounce of resistance to overcome. Pearly Stevens' enjoyment of her struggle made it an even harder result to achieve.

'As you are probably aware, Stevens,' Rochester said. 'The remains of a young woman has been found in a grave in Thatcher's Lot—'

'Such a lawless society now, don't you think? But I expect it has its good side, Constable. It keeps you lot busy. And therefore keeps unemployment down.'

Rochester ignored the interruption.

'We have information that Thatcher's Lot was a stomping ground of yours in your early years of . . .' Helen Rochester snorted. 'Your rise in the Loston community as a *business* man.'

Stevens' smile did not fully manage to hide the poison behind it. Rochester did nothing to hide her pleasure at this small victory. She went on:

'Coming straight to the point. You dealt drugs there, Stevens.'

Pearly Stevens yawned theatrically. 'And your evidence, Constable?' He rolled his eyes and put his hand to his mouth in a camp fashion. 'Oh, dear. You haven't. Silly girl. This is all rather tiresome, re-hashing old accusations.' His eyes became points of flint. 'The police, though ever the triers, have failed on several occasions in the past to prove any of these silly and outrageous allegations. I can only assume, now that once more you're prepared to trot out this rubbish again, that the police are going through a quiet phase and someone somewhere wants you to justify your existence. Well, I'd be the last to want to see redundancy in the Loston Constabulary.'

'With you above ground,' Brian Scuttle snapped, 'redundancy will never be a worry, Stevens.'

'Oh, dear me,' Stevens groaned. 'Me thinks the bulldog has slipped its leash, Constable.'

Above all else at that precise moment, DC Helen Rochester wanted to scream at her partner, 'Shut it!' If looks could kill, Brian Scuttle would have been struck down instantly.

'Let's get back to your former activities in Thatcher's Lot, Stevens,' Rochester said.

'Former implies that these activities you are so preoccupied with have some basis in fact. Which I have denied before and do so again now most vehemently. And I must object in the strongest possible terms, Constable Rochester. This is nothing more than police harassment.'

Again, Helen Rochester ignored Pearly Stevens' objections. But she knew how close to the wind she was sailing.

'Did you know a woman by the name of Linda Wright?'

'Doesn't ring a bell.'

'She was a drug addict—'

'Poor thing.'

'We have good reason to believe that you were her supplier, Stevens.'

Pearly Stevens looked at her with a face set in stone. 'I think it would be preferable at this point in our little chat if I were to refer you to my solicitor, Constable Rochester. Shall I give him a call to come round?'

'That to me sounds like you were Linda Wright's supplier, Stevens.'

'I've grown weary of this silliness, Constable.'

'Then let's try some other silliness, shall we?'

'And if I don't feel like indulging you?'

'Well, we can always adjourn to the station.'

'You've no good reason to take me in,' Stevens sneered.

'No, that's true. But there just might be a photographer from the *Loston Echo* hanging about the station at that time.'

George 'Pearly' Stevens' look would have frightened the devil. 'That, Constable, is blackmail.'

'Something you're probably quite an expert on, Stevens. I'm sure that when all those silly well-to-dos were cavorting around the Blue Stocking, you took full advantage of their indiscretions.'

Helen Rochester held his gaze, unflinching.

'Now, I know, like the good citizen you are, you'll want to help the police, Mr Stevens.'

'It's my duty as a good citizen, isn't it, Constable?'

'You had a DJ at the club – David Dees.'

'What about him? A talented man, Dees. He was a fantastic drag queen. Brought the house down regularly. Married a rich woman, has he? He tried hard enough to hook one.'

'A rich woman like Elinor Roebuck, for example.'

'She wasn't a rich woman. But she did have the potential to be, once the olds popped their clogs. But Dees was not a patient man. He wanted everything right now. So, with that in mind, Elinor had her uses.'

'Like?'

'She was a door.'

'A door?' PC Brian Scuttle said.

'Yeah. A door to real riches.' Pearly Stevens shook his head. 'You lot aren't the brightest, are you?'

'We're always willing to be educated,' Rochester said.

'Dees used Elinor Roebuck to get to her old lady.'

'Emily Roebuck and David Dees?'

'Close your mouth, Constable,' Stevens mocked. 'You'll catch flies.'

'But our information is that Emily Roebuck hated the living sight of Dees. She ran him out of the house when he turned up there with Elinor.'

'The green-eyed monster, eh? Dees thought it was all so hilarious. He joined the gym where Emily Roebuck worked out. Did you see her? She has more muscles that Arnold Schwarzenegger. Ten minutes in the gym, and fifty in the back of her Merc.' Stevens laughed. 'And just in case there was a hitch in securing the Roebuck fortune, Dees had a second string to his bow – Susan Finch. Probably even more dosh than the Roebucks.'

'Mr Dees was a busy man,' Rochester observed, deadpan.

'Susan Finch's mum also?' Brian Scuttle intoned, in a voice that Helen Rochester could not decide was awe or admiration. 'What kind of a frigging diet did this bloke have?'

'No,' Stevens said. 'Mrs Finch, quoting Dees, was as immovable as Everest. And' – he chuckled – 'harder to climb. Now I really am out of information and goodwill, Constable,' he told Helen Rochester. 'Good citizenry can be so exhausting.'

'Just bear with me for a moment, Stevens—'

'Would that be *bear* or *bare*?' Stevens asked mischievously. 'Just to avoid any confusion that could land me in court.'

Rochester ignored the jibe.

'At any time did Emily Roebuck have Dees to the house, when she was alone?'

'Couldn't say. But I suppose it's reasonable to think that she might have. Dees told me that she couldn't get enough. Now, you're thinking that Elinor Roebuck walked in and caught them banging away for England.

'Mummy thought she'd tell Daddy and she'd be out on her ear, probably penniless. Or Dees saw a fortune fading into the sunset. Which would make the perfect motive for murder for either or both.'

George 'Pearly' Stevens sighed.

'You know, in my silly youth I thought about becoming a copper. Maybe I'd have had a talent for it, don't you think? But I just don't look good in a uniform.'

'Where's this Dees fellow now?'

'Ireland. Beara Peninsula. He took to the brush,' Stevens laughed uproariously. 'A natural follow on from strokes, isn't it?'

'He became an artist?' Scuttle enquired.

'Nothing as grand, I'm afraid. House painting.'

'What's his actual address?'

'I'm not *Encylopedia Britannica*,' Stevens groused. 'It's Ireland. Pocket-sized and bloody nosy. When you hit the peninsula, ask. Check the local supermarket. His card will probably be on the noticeboard. Failing all of that check with the local plod.

'You pair would need a great deal of retraining. It would make people like me feel a lot safer in their beds.'

'Do you have a photograph of David Dees?'

'We weren't that close,' he told Helen Rochester.

'If you weren't, he seemed to confide in you a lot.'

Stevens arched an eyebrow.

Rochester looked around the walls of the apartment, and scattered among the paintings (she was no expert, but Rochester reckoned that there was a couple of old masters in there, mixed with the newer kids of the canvas) were framed photographs of events and personalities at the Blue Stocking Club.

'You seem fond of mementos. So I'm sure you've got a picture of Dees around somewhere, Mr Stevens?'

'You're a very demanding woman, Constable,' he said. He went to the drawer of a desk and took from it a black and white photograph of Dees in drag. 'Dees said he photographed better in black and white.' He handed the picture over.

Helen Rochester looked at the photograph.

'Handsome bastard, behind all that make-up,' Stevens commented.

'Fancied him, did you?' Scuttle said.

Stevens pouted his lips. 'I prefer men in uniform, copper.'

David Dees' handsomeness was of no interest to DC Helen Rochester. But the shoulder bag he had slung over his shoulder as part of his Miss Tarty-Tawdrey act was. It was a handbag with its strap attached to two large brass rings.

Just like the strap that was found in Elinor Roebuck's grave.

Before leaving, Rochester had a sudden and a very intuitive idea.

'Oh, nearly forgot. PC Roger Bennett said to say hello, Stevens.'

'You have me at a disadvantage, Constable,' he said, suavely, but not before there was a second's flicker of alarm in his eyes. Pearly Stevens had come as close to being caught off guard as he ever would be.

'He's on the mend,' Rochester said.

'Delighted for him,' Stevens said with aplomb, fully recovered from his whisker of hesitation.

'Almost ready to be interviewed about his unfortunate meeting with a baseball bat.'

'Oh, dear. How very distressing for him. Though I've not had the pleasure of the gentleman's acquaintance, do please pass on my kind regards.'

WPC Anne Fenning, given the task of checking on the backgrounds of the people in the missing women's circle, looked at her computer screen with a degree of excitement. It was a caution about soliciting a woman for prostitution. The woman's name was Linda Wright nothing surprising there. However, the man's name came as a bolt out of the blue. And that name was: Cyril Roebuck.

CHAPTER THIRTEEN

Liv Benson kept stirring her tea fit to wear the china tea cup brittle. 'Melissa wasn't feeling very well,' she explained. 'She's been suffering from depression of late. Marital troubles, I think, though she didn't specfically come out with it. Personally, I never thought Simon and she were suited from the start.'

'They quarrelled?' Andy Lukeson asked.

'No, not in a screaming-match way. It was more or less . . .' Liv Benson became thoughtful. 'Well, a state of truce, I suppose. You know, they didn't talk much. And always seemed to be just on the right side of an argument.'

'For how long has this been going on?'

'The last year or so.'

'Any known reason for this ill feeling?'

'Like I said, Melissa didn't talk about it much. The odd hint that things between her and Simon were not as they should be. But she'd always say, "I'm sure it'll all work out for the best".' She gave a sad little laugh. 'Melissa, the eternal optimist.'

'Depression and optimism are strange bedfellows,' Sally Speckle observed.

'Well, for a while past Melissa was either over the moon or under a cloud.'

She began stirring the tea again after a brief pause.

'Mr Scott, he's not around?' Lukeson enquired.

'I've been trying to contact him. He has his mobile on the message minder. I contacted the college but they said he'd left.'

'What college would that be, Ms Benson?' the DI enquired.

'Loston College. Simon is the deputy head there. And it's expected that he'll be the head master when Mr Clarence, the present head, retires next month. Lives for the place, does Simon. I think the imbalance between college and home life was the main cause of the rift in his marriage.

'Melissa wasn't the ambitious type, really. She was content to plod along. Let tomorrow take care of itself was her motto. And Simon wanted to reach the pinnacle of his profession.'

'And becoming the headmaster at Loston College would be this pinnacle?' Speckle asked.

'Far from it, Inspector. Simon's sights were set much higher than that. Loston College was not the end, rather it was a springboard to reach loftier heights.'

'Did the college say where Mr Scott had gone?'

'They said he was feeling unwell and had gone to see his GP.'

'And his GP would be?' Lukeson asked.

'Dr Williams. His surgery is on Albert Street. Oh, heavens.' Liv Benson slapped her forehead with her hand. 'I'm an idiot. If I'd phoned Dr Williams' surgery Simon would have been there.'

'Perhaps you'd do that now, Ms Benson,' Speckle suggested.

She took her mobile from her anorak pocket and punched out a number. Waited for a moment. Then: 'Alice, Liv Benson. Is Simon Scott there? No? Well, thanks anyway. Yes, I've been meaning to get in for that cholesterol test .. Not now, Alice.'

She broke the connection.

'That's odd. Alice, Dr Williams' receptionist, says Simon's never been.' The implication of Simon Scott's non-attendance at the doctor's surgery and his mysterious absence from Loston College began to sink in. 'There must be a perfectly good explanation, don't you think?' she said, seeking reassurance.

'I'm sure there is,' Speckle said, Alec Balson's description of Melissa Scott's murderer ringing in her ears.

'*Knife. Under the ribs and up into the heart with considerable force.*'

'Perhaps if you gave us a description of Mr Scott, Ms

Benson,' the DI suggested kindly. 'One of our cars might spot him.'

Clever girl, Andy Lukeson thought. Much more subtle that a crude question like, 'Is Mr Scott a big muscular man who could shove a blade forcefully under the ribs and up into your sister's heart?'

'Yes, of course,' Liv Benson immediately agreed, unconcerned, evidence of how slickly Sally Speckle's suggestion had been made. 'He's just under six feet tall. Broad shouldered. Looks more like a builder's labourer than a schoolmaster. Fair hair, inclined to curl at the end. Blue eyes with a greenish tinge.'

'Perfect,' Speckle said, exchanging a quick glance with Andy Lukeson, and thinking the same as he was. Liv Benson's description of Simon Scott had been delivered softly; in fact as close to dreamy as didn't matter. Did Liv Benson covet her sister's husband? Or had it gone much further than that?

She summoned the PC who had been first on the scene and passed on the description. 'Get it out on air right away.'

The knives in the kitchen flat all seemed to be present and correct. Twelve slots on the block, twelve knives, including the bread knife, all the same type. Cutlery knives could, by Balson's conclusion, be ruled out. But there were, that Speckle could recall offhand, four hardware stores in Loston where a kitchen knife could be purchased. But more likely, if Scott had planned the murder, he would have been clever enough to have gone well away from Loston to procure the murder weapon.

Having in mind Liv Benson's detailed description of Simon Scott, Sally Speckle enquired, conversationally, 'You and Simon Scott get on well, do you?'

'Yes.'

'Would you describe your relationship as friendly?'

Liv Benson looked hard at Sally Speckle. 'What are you getting at?'

'Getting at, Ms Benson?'

The sudden shifty unease in Liv Benson confirmed Speckle and Lukeson's suspicions. The DI went for the jugular.

'Are you having an affair with Simon Scott, Ms Benson?'

'How dare you!'

'These things are easily checked out,' Speckle said.

Liv Benson's gaze shifted away from Speckle's.

'Were you the reason for the trouble between your sister and her husband, Ms Benson?' Andy Lukeson enquired bluntly.

'No,' she protested, but her protest lacked conviction. Her shoulders slumped and she deflated like a rubber doll whose plug had been pulled. 'We were getting ready to tell Melissa, as soon as Simon had secured the headmaster's post. We were only waiting because the break-up of his marriage would have ruined his chance of being appointed. The board of governors of the college are a conservative bunch, three canons on the board. Two C of E and one RC – different theologically but bedfellows in matters moral.

'It just happened. What else can I say. I didn't plan on falling in love with Simon. But being honest, there had always been a spark waiting to ignite the fire since Melissa first introduced him to me. I ignored it. Hoped it would go away. But it didn't.

'Then one evening when I called, Melissa was out and . . .'

She held her head in her hands. Speckle and Lukeson waited.

'Anyway, about an hour ago, Melissa phoned me. Said that she had found a letter from me to Simon. She said that she was going to contact the board of governors and sink his chance of getting the headmaster's job. I pleaded with her, but she slammed down the phone on me.'

'Did you contact Mr Scott with the news?' Lukeson asked.

'I phoned, but like I said, I couldn't make contact with him.'

'Do you know if Mrs Scott contacted the board of governors?'

'I don't know.'

'Perhaps she did, and that's why Mr Scott left the college. And he might have come here to have it out with Melissa.'

'Simon wouldn't swat a fly!'

'He might if that fly had cost him his promotion. Has Mr Scott a temper? Is he impulsive?'

Liv Benson cast her eyes down.

'Has he ever been violent towards your sister?'

'Slapped her once or twice,' she admitted quietly. 'Nothing serious. Simon's temper was short-lived, Sergeant.'

'Often the most furious type,' Lukeson said.

'What I mean is that by the time he reached here, he'd have cooled down.'

Andy Lukeson fished. 'Did he seem calm when you saw him, Ms Benson?'

'Yes, he did,' she answered, without thinking, and then as quiet as a church mouse: 'He drove off as I arrived.'

'You said your sister phoned you, right?' Sally Speckle checked.

'Yes.'

'Would it not have been easier for you to phone her back when she hung up on you instead of coming round?'

'I waited a while. I needed time to think. Then I did phone back. But she was engaged.'

'Phoning the college, you think?'

Liv Benson shrugged.

'I was completely on edge. I couldn't sit still. So I came round to talk things through. To see if I could make Melissa see sense. She had long ago stopped loving Simon. She told me so. So why was she being so vindictive and making such a bloody fuss?'

'You were angry when you arrived here, then?' Speckle said.

'Fit to be tied,' she admitted honestly, and added with equal candour, 'but not in a mood to murder, Inspector.'

Andy Lukeson took up the questioning. 'Did your sister phone you from the landline phone?'

'Yes. She couldn't abide mobiles. Had this wacky idea that they made your hair fall out.'

'Back in a mo,' Lukeson told Speckle.

The DS returned to Melissa Scott's flat, picked up the phone, and used redial to recall the last number called. The phone rang out for quite awhile before a gruff male voice answered:

'Yeah. What do you want?'

Lukeson could hear the sound of traffic in the background, and knew the answer to his question before he asked it. 'Is that a public phonebox?'

'Don't you know where you're calling?' the man asked, annoyed.

'Please, it's important that I know.'

'Yeah. It's a public phonebox,' the man confirmed.

'Where?'

'The corner of Essex Street.'

The corner of the street in which Melissa Scott's flat was situated.

'That it?'

'Yes. Thank you.'

'Welcome, I'm sure.'

He went back to the flat across the way where Liv Benson had been taken in after finding her sister.

'What time did you phone your sister, when you got her engaged?' he enquired of her.

'About eleven o'clock.'

He returned to Melissa Scott's flat and phoned the contact number the police had with the telephone company. 'Hello, DS Andy Lukeson Loston CID. I'd like to check if the number I'm phoning from was called from a payphone at the corner of Essex Street about eleven o'clock this morning?' After a couple of minutes waiting: 'Thank you very much. And was there a call from this number to Loston College this morning?'

Information acquired, he beckoned to Sally Speckle to join him on the landing.

'Someone phoned Melissa Scott from the payphone on the corner of this street at 10.59 this morning. Then she phoned back. I checked redial. It was the payphone.

'I think Melissa Scott phoned her killer. And when the killer arrived here, he or she phoned her back from the payphone to cancel out the redial facility on Scott's phone, which could have revealed the killer, if Scott had not phoned someone else after she had phoned her murderer. By getting her to phone back the payphone, that became the last number called.

'But a check on the calls made would reveal the numbers Melissa Scott had phoned anyway, Andy. So why would the killer go to all this rigmarole?'

'Perhaps we'd never have any reason to check, Sally. And if we did, by the time we got round to it, the person phoned by Melissa Scott would have had time to calm down and concoct a reasonable story for why Melissa Scott had phoned. But if we activated the recall facility, we'd be right back to the killer a short time after he or she had murdered Scott. The killer would not have had the time to calm down and would likely be nervous and vulnerable.'

DI Sally Speckle smiled. 'Who's a clever boy, then.'

'And Melissa Scott did phone Loston College, fifteen minutes before the call from the payphone.'

On leaving Pearly Stevens' penthouse, Brian Scuttle's brow furrowed. 'What was all that about Roger Bennett, then?' he enquired of Helen Rochester.

'A spur of the moment idea.'

'What idea?'

'Well, Stevens has a finger in every dirty pie around, right?'

'Right.'

'So, I figured there was a very good chance that he was involved in the illegal betting that's been Roger Bennett's downfall.'

'Makes sense,' Brian Scuttle agreed.

'So I thought why not pretend that Bennett had mentioned him. See Stevens' reaction. And he lost his Ibiza tan for a second before he recovered.'

'That was a bloody dangerous game to play,' Scuttle said. 'What if Stevens has bought into your scheme? He's liable to send his thugs round to the hospital to pay Roger a visit.'

'And that's why we have to move fast and clear the plan I have in mind with our DI.'

'What plan would that be?'

Helen Rochester grinned. 'The plan in which you'll play the starring role, of course, Brian.'

'Eh?'

CHAPTER FOURTEEN

'Melissa Scott phones the college and puts in the poison. Enraged, Scott comes home and murders his wife? It can't be that easy, can it?' DI Sally Speckle asked Andy Lukeson.

'Sometimes it is. Most murders, other than nutter killings, are committed by someone close to the victim. So statistics would favour that solution. However, there's also Melissa Scott's sister to consider as the killer.

'Telling your sister that you're running off with her husband is the stuff of rage. Feeling guilty, or more likely fearing Melissa sinking her lover's boat, Liv Benson comes round to pour oil on troubled waters. All hell breaks loose and—'

'That can't be, Andy. One, pouring oil on troubled waters means that Melissa would have admitted her and there would have been argy-bargy. But the theory so far is that Melissa opened the door to her murderer and the killer struck immediately. That would mean that there was never any intention of pouring oil on troubled waters, because Liv Benson would have had to come prepared. So her intention would be to murder Melissa and not talk to her.'

'But that's all it is at this stage – a theory. Maybe Benson was leaving when she stabbed her sister. The same could apply to Scott.'

'And the murder weapon? Where did that come from? We checked the kitchen knives and they're all there, Andy. Twelve slots on the block, twelve knives, same type, including the bread knife. And cutlery knives would not match the wound.

'There could have been another knife hanging about,' Lukeson said without conviction.

Sally Speckle was also unconvinced. 'There's something else that doesn't fit. Alec Balson said that Melissa Scott had been stabbed with force – considerable force – and . . .'

'Liv Benson is a weakling.'

'I suspect she's probably anorexic or bulimic. And she's at least six inches smaller than her sister.'

'So we're back to the enraged husband.'

'He's the more likely bet. Unless there was more going on in Melissa Scott's life than we know about. And it seems that Simon Scott's done a runner.'

DI Sally Speckle and DS Andy Lukeson returned from the landing to resume the questioning of Liv Benson.

*

Arbour Square was a row of Georgian houses that were slowly losing the battle against the march of time and were going the route of all such properties, first to flats, then to flats of a lower standard, then to dosshouse status, and finally demolition. Number sixteen was one of two houses that were reasonably well kept, but broken windows on the top floor of number fifteen, letting in rain and damp, would soon bring its neighbour to the same state of delapidation. DC Charlie Johnson and WPC Sue Blake went up the steps, and Johnson used the brass knocker to announce their presence.

'Yes?' enquired the harassed-looking woman who answered.

'Miss Armstrong?' Johnson asked.

'Yes. I'm Hilda Armstrong.'

Johnson showed his warrant card. 'And my colleague is WPC Sue Blake.'

'Margaret!' a man's voice wailed from inside the house.

'My father,' Hilda Armstrong explained. 'He's not very well. What is it you want?'

'Margaret!'

'Coming, Dad,' she called back into the house. 'Alzheimer's. God only knows who Margaret is. Probably some old girlfriend.'

'We've come to talk to your father,' Charlie Johnson said.

'Talk to Dad?' She said it as if she had discovered a couple of lunatics on her doorstep. 'Only a couple of minutes before you called I was Lucy. And before that I was Janet.'

'Mary!'

She smiled sadly. 'I often wonder how many girlfriends he had.' She shrugged. 'Maybe they were mistresses.'

'Mary!'

'I'm coming now, Dad. How could my father help you? Most of the time, except for the odd lucid spell that lasts minutes or more likely seconds, he's off in some other place.'

'We just wanted to ask him about a couple of his former patients,' Johnson said.

'Then I suggest you contact Mr Bernstein, the dentist who took over my father's practice. He should—'

'We've already spoken to Mr Bernstein, Miss Armstrong.'

The Beatles classic 'All You Need Is Love' came from inside the house, sung in a high-pitched croak.

'Although he was thirty-three when the Fab Four were fighting off hordes of screaming women, my father was quite a fan.'

The song became garbled and petered out and the words escaped Jack Armstrong.

'I'm sorry,' Johnson said. 'I'm sure you don't need us—'

'Who are you?' A man, presumably Armstrong, sprang

out of a room at the end of the dark panelled hall. 'Call the police, Alice,' he ranted.

Hilda Armstrong hurried to him.

'These are the police, Dad,' she told him.

'What have you done, woman?' he asked, quite lucidly.

'Nothing, Dad. Now do calm yourself.'

'Alice didn't bring me my tea,' he said sadly, slipping back into wherever he had momentarily come from. 'Why didn't Alice bring me my tea?'

'She'll bring it to you shortly. Now you go and sit down and rest yourself.'

As she escorted him back into the room, Armstrong turned and pointed at Charlie Johnson. 'I know you. You're John Lennon.'

'All You Need Is Love' began again, plaintively.

Hilda Armstrong poked her head out of the room door. 'Please come in. There's quite a draught and he catches cold easily now.'

'We're wasting our time, Charlie,' Sue Blake whispered when Johnson did as Hilda Armstrong requested of them.

'We don't want to give offence, Sue,' Johnson said in a whispered aside. 'We'll stay a minute or two and then leave.'

'Please.' Hilda Armstrong waved them into the sitting-room.

When they returned, having had time to think, Liv Benson looked at Speckle and Lukeson apprehensively.

'I've told you everything,' she said defensively. 'I don't know what more I can tell you.'

Speckle's mobile rang. 'Yes? I see. I'll be along shortly.'

Liv Benson's eyes lit with alarm. 'Simon?'

'Yes.'

'Is he OK?' Her voice reeked of anxiety. 'Where was he?'

'Uniform picked him up at the railway station.'

'That doesn't make sense. Simon hates train travel.'

'He probably thought that his car would be spotted, I imagine,' Speckle said.

'Oh, good grief,' Benson wailed. 'Has he been arrested?'

'He's wanted for questioning in connection with his wife's murder, Ms Benson.'

'Can I see him? Now?'

'I don't think that would be possible.'

'Will he have a solicitor?'

'Do you think he'll need a solicitor?'

'You' – her gaze included Andy Lukeson – 'think he murdered Melissa. Of course he'll need a solicitor.'

'If Mr Scott requests that a solictor should be present then he will get one, either his own or one will be appointed to advise him,' the DI explained.

'Someone else murdered Melissa.'

'Someone else,' Andy Lukeson said. 'Who and why, Ms Benson?'

'Someone out of Melissa's past.'

'Her past? Did she know people who might be potential killers in her past?'

'When she was younger, Melissa ran with a pretty wild bunch. One of her friends was murdered,' she stated.

Speckle and Lukeson exchanged glances.

'When I found Melissa I noticed the *Loston Echo* on the kitchen table. Her coffee mug was on it, so she must have been reading that awful story about the woman's skeleton that was found in Thatcher's Lot. She probably thought that it was a woman called Elinor Roebuck, you see.'

'She and Elinor Roebuck were friends?'

'Yes.'

'Did Melissa say that she had been murdered?'

'No.' Liv Benson wrung her hands. 'When I said murdered, it was an assumption on my part instead of a fact.'

Jack Armstrong watched as DC Charlie Johnson and WPC Sue Blake came into the room, sinking deeper into the armchair he sat on as if trying to make himself invisible.

'He thinks you're Martians,' his daughter explained. 'Keeps on about Martians landing to kidnap humans for experimentation. Along with being a big Beatles fan, he was also an avid reader of science fiction. These people are here for a chat, Dad. Wouldn't you like to chat?'

Armstrong did not answer; he simply sank further into the armchair.

'You'll get nothing out of him today. It's a bloody cruel

disease. Some days he remembers a lot, even me,' Hilda Armstrong said sadly. 'Calls me Dotspot. That's what he used to call me when I was a freckle-faced child.'

Tears welled up in her eyes as memories of times past flooded back and she hurriedly brushed them away.

'I'll get your tea now, Dad,' she said.

'You'll never win, you know,' Armstrong said authoritatively, sitting bolt upright in his chair. 'Never, damn you!'

'I'll be right back,' Hilda Armstrong said.

When she had gone, Armstrong's authority slipped away and he returned to huddling in the armchair, whimpering.

'What a horrible illness,' Sue Blake said, shrinking back from Armstrong as he stretched out a hand to take hers in his.

'Take his hand,' Charlie Johnson said. 'Go on. He must think you're a friend. Someone from the past. It would be cruel to disappoint him.'

Trembling, Sue Blake took Jack Armstrong's bony hand in hers.

'You're shivering, my dear,' he said, lucidly. 'You must be cold.'

'It's a little chilly,' Blake said.

'We can't have that, Miriam,' he said fondly. 'I'll turn on the gas fire.'

Sue Blake looked with alarm at Johnson as Armstrong went and turned on the gas fire, searching his pockets for a match to light it.

'I've no bloody matches,' he said. He called out. 'Hilda.'

Footsteps hurried along the hall.

'I've no bloody matches,' Armstrong repeated. 'And our guests are cold.'

'I'll light the fire, Dad.'

'Good girl.'

Armstrong went and sat down in his armchair. 'Can't have our guests catch cold.'

Hilda Armstrong's eyes glowed with sheer love.

'No. That would never do, Dad.'

Armstrong looked at Sue Blake and Charlie Johnson, and Johnson could see the light fade from his eyes and, fearful again, he huddled into the armchair. His daughter was heartbroken.

'That's the first time in over a year he's called me Hilda.'

'Will Alice be bringing tea soon?' Jack Armstrong asked in a childlike voice.

'Alice was our maid. That's what Alzheimer's does,' Hilda Armstrong said bitterly. 'Leaves one with nothing but ghosts from the past. I shouldn't keep you, but if you could wait until I get back.'

'Of course,' Charlie Johnson said.

Hilda Armstrong went and extinguished the gas fire again. 'Safer,' she said.

Charlie Johnson and Sue Blake sat as quiet as church mice, fearing that any movement might upset Jack Armstrong.

'Ask him about Elinor Roebuck,' Sue Blake said quietly.

Johnson shook his head. 'Waste of time, Sue.'

Hilda Armstrong came back with the tea tray.

'Won't you join us?'

'Best be off,' Charlie Johnson said. 'We'll see oursleves out. Bye. Sorry for disturbing you.'

'No. Sorry Dad couldn't help you.'

' 'Bye, Miriam,' Armstrong said softly, his befuddled eyes filled with memories.

'Miriam was my mum,' Hilda explained. 'She died ten years ago.'

'Goodbye, *Jack*,' Sue Blake said.

'I've always loved you, you know,' Armstrong said. 'Always will.'

'Thanks,' Hilda Armstrong said.

They were walking along the hall to the front door when they stopped on hearing a commotion. 'Dad,' Hilda Armstrong pleaded. 'Please, don't get yourself so worked up. It's not good for you.'

Jack Armstrong dashed out of the sitting-room into the hall, and declared with absolute lucidity, 'Elinor Roebuck. The young woman wanted to know about Elinor Roebuck. Well, she was pregnant when she went missing. I know because a couple of days before she came to my surgery to have some work done. And she asked me if there was any danger to her baby. There wasn't, of course.'

Astounded, Charlie Johnson asked, 'Did Elinor say

who the father was?'

'What?'

'I asked if—'

'Who are these people, Alice?' he asked Hilda Armstrong. 'Get rid of them.' He stormed back into the sitting-room.

'Sorry. There'll be no point in asking him any more questions now. What was it you wanted anyway?'

'We came to ask your father about two of his former patients – if he might have dental records we need in connection with an ongoing inquiry,' Charlie Johnson explained.

'Oh, maybe I can help you with those.'

'You can?'

'When Dad retired and sold the practice, being the careful man that he is ... was, he made copies of all of his records, just in case something legal might come up later when dates would be of the utmost importance in proving or disproving a point.

'There are boxes of them down in the basement. Shall I get the key?'

Ten minutes later, DC Charlie Johnson left with Elinor Roebuck and Susan Finch's dental records.

'Melissa and Elinor were friends,' Liv Benson said. 'They met in the Blue Stocking Club. Spent almost every night there. Me, I didn't fancy it at all. Sleazy, I thought. When it closed, Melissa was terribly cut up about it. She broke up with Frank around that time, and that didn't help at all.'

'Frank?' Lukeson queried.

'Melissa's boyfriend of the time, Frank Boyd.'

'How did Boyd get on with Elinor Roebuck?'

'Oh, they hit it off the first time they met. Before Melissa and Frank broke up, there was talk of Elinor going on holiday with them.'

'Elinor Roebuck and Frank Boyd were close, then?'

'Peas in a pod, really.' Liv Benson frowned, obviously thinking about Andy Lukeson's question and her own reply. 'There was nothing going on between Frank Boyd and Elinor Roebuck, if that's what you're thinking,' she said. 'Nothing.'

DI Sally Speckle picked up the questioning. 'How can you be so sure?'

'Well, I can't be positive, of course. But I think I'd have known. Frank Boyd was the kind of man whose thoughts and emotions showed on his face. Like I said, I'd have known.'

'Maybe your sister might have seen it differently. Might Elinor Roebuck be the reason that your sister broke up with Boyd? How was the relationship between Elinor and Melissa, post Frank Boyd, Ms Benson?'

'Not as close as it had been, but that was because soon after Melissa broke up with Frank the Blue Stocking closed. So naturally they would not be seeing as much of each other. And, anyway, Melissa would have said if

Frank was seeing Elinor.'

'Your sister confided in you a lot?'

'We had regular chinwags, yes. And, as I recall, at the time Elinor Roebuck was dating Da Dees.'

'You mean David Dees?' Lukeson checked.

'Yes. But the in crowd at the Blue Stocking called him Da, because he was completely grey. It was a club joke.'

'Do you know where Frank Boyd is now?'

Liv Benson shook her head. 'One day he was all over the place, and the next day he wasn't. At least that's how it seemed back then. I think Melissa said something about him having gone back home.'

'And where was home?'

'Scotland. Kirkcaldy seems to ring a bell.'

Sally Speckle's mobile rang. 'Sorry.'

'I've found a partial, Sally,' the fingerprint officer said. 'On a ring she was wearing on her right hand. It's a man's signet ring, probably her father's – my sister wore our father's signet ring when he passed on. It's smooth from wear so the print is very good. It could be that the killer shook hands with the victim.'

'Thanks, Herb.'

Speckle took a moment to think before resuming the questioning of Liv Benson. Her sister would not have shaken hands with Melissa Scott. But in an act of pleading she might have clasped her sister's hands in hers. And perhaps Simon Scott had done the same?

'I mean, come to think of it, Melissa and Elinor must

still have been friends,' Liv Benson was saying to Andy Lukeson. 'Why else would Melissa go to meet Elinor in Thatcher's Lot on the day Elinor went missing?'

DI Sally Speckle spun round.

CHAPTER FIFTEEN

In the absence of her DI and DS, who were attending at the scene of a murder, WPC Anne Fenning sought out the next senior officer on the team and that was DC Charlie Johnson.

'I think you'd better look at this, Charlie,' she said.

Johnson, indulging his passion for Yorkshire pudding in the station canteen ('About the only thing even half edible,' had been his often-voiced opinion about the canteen fare), grudgingly took the computer printout from Fenning. 'Can't it wait?' he grumbled.

'That's your decision to make,' Fenning said huffily, Johnson's attitude getting up her nose. 'But with the DI and the sarge not here, I'm obliged to pass it to you.'

'Helen Rochester is a DC, too, you know.'

'But you're senior.'

'By less than a month.'

'Still senior,' said WPC Anne Fenning. Enjoying her

moment of triumph, she dropped the printout on the table. 'That makes this your baby, Charlie.'

'Elinor Roebuck phoned Melissa that afternoon,' Liv Benson explained. 'I was right here when she called. Melissa had to calm her down. Elinor was in a right old state. Melissa said that she'd have to go out to Thatcher's Lot to meet Elinor right away.'

'Did Melissa say what had got Elinor Roebuck into a state?'

'All Melissa would say was that it was to do with David Dees.'

'Why Thatcher's Lot?' Speckle queried.

'I asked Melissa the same question, and she told me that the Lot was the safest place to talk because it would be the last place that anyone would expect Elinor to be. Apparently, Elinor Roebuck suffered from chronic hayfever, and the Lot would be the last place anyone would look for her. It was July.

'Melissa waited around for a while, but when Elinor didn't turn up she thought that she had changed her mind and wasn't coming.'

'Did your sister tell the police about this meeting?' Lukeson asked. 'Because I don't recall seeing anything about it in the case file.'

'No.'

'Why not?'

'Well, at the time, Melissa thought that Elinor had just

decided to fly the coop and that she'd be back when she was good and ready. She'd gone off like that a time or two before, as I understood. Then, later, Melissa was afraid of the trouble she might get herself into with you lot by speaking out. Understandable, isn't it.'

'Bloody foolish more like,' Andy Lukeson said. 'Withholding information that might have made all the difference.'

'I know. That worried Mel. And now this skeleton that was found in Thatcher's Lot obviously opened it all up for Melissa again.'

'Only this time it won't worry her, will it?' Lukeson said, immediately regretting the insensitivity of his remarks.

His outburst, though understandable, took Sally Speckle by surprise because it was not in Andy Lukeson's nature to be vindictive. But, feeling the same frustration, she might have been the one to have spoken out. In effect, it may very well have been Melissa Scott's stupid silence that had now got her killed. And the person who went to the trouble of phoning from the payphone was probably her killer. But why would Melissa Scott have phoned the killer in the first place? Presumably because she did not know that this person was Elinor Roebuck's murderer. Had she, she would have surely realized the danger she was putting herself in. Unless, of course, this person was a friend and Melissa thought there was no threat to her? Or she did not realize the can of worms her phone call would open?

After a tense stand-off, Liv Benson said, 'Melissa said that there was an old geezer in Thatcher's Lot. She didn't take any notice at the time.'

'Did Melissa say anything else about this man?' Speckle enquired.

'Like what?'

'Did she mention anything about him? Like his height? Colour of hair? Was he bald? Fat? Thin?'

A description had been too much to hope for. However, with a case that was going round in ever wider circles, Sally Speckle had dared to hope.

'But Melissa did say that he had a metal detector.'

An old geezer. A metal detector. Fred White?

'When can I see Simon?'

'Not for a while yet, I'm afraid,' Speckle said. 'Not until we talk to him first.'

'He'll be very upset. He'll need me to be with him.'

'Sorry. But not until we talk to him first,' Sally Speckle repeated, her mind totally occupied with the possibility that Fred White was Elinor Roebuck's killer.

Andy Lukeson went to fetch the PC who had been first on the scene. Returning he said, 'This officer will take your written statement, Ms Benson. Oh, and we'd like your cooperation in fingerprinting you.'

'Why? I was a frequent visitor. My fingerprints will be all over the flat.'

Again, that old police standby. 'Just routine, Ms Benson.'

*

DC Charlie Johnson decided to savour one more mouthful of the spicy Yorkshire pudding before he bothered with the printout WPC Anne Fenning had left on the table. 'Bloody marvellous,' he said, letting the Yorkshire pudding slide down his throat. 'Just like Mum used to make.'

Now he picked up the printout, and the Yorkshire pudding did a somersault.

CHAPTER SIXTEEN

'Well done, Anne,' DI Sally Speckle complimented WPC Anne Fenning. 'Good work unearthing Cyril Roebuck's fondness for kerb crawling and the attempted pick-up of Linda Wright. Being followed up, is it?'

'Charlie Johnson's on it, boss.'

Sally Speckle shook her head. 'A dark horse, our Cyril. Didn't think he was the type, frankly.'

'It was his second caution,' Fenning said, having since unearthed another offence of kerb crawling over in Brigham, only two months before. 'Another young girl. So how hasn't Roebuck ended up in court?'

'Friends in high places?'

Fenning doubted. 'Does that really happen, do you think?'

'What was the age of the girl over in Brigham?'

'Fourteen.'

'Linda Wright was on the game at thirteen. I wonder if

Roebuck's was a repeat visit? And I wonder if Roebuck has a fondness for young girls, as distinct from young prostitutes?'

'I checked with the officer over in Brigham, the one from here packed it all in last year. He says that Roebuck claimed that he was fooled by the young girl's appearance and thought she was much older. He says that Roebuck could have a point. Tarted up, they can look older.'

Speckle shook her head again. 'Roebuck looks such an innocent, grandfather type.'

'That's what fools a lot of kids. Look like a dragon and they run. Takes all sorts,' Anne Fenning said philosophically. 'There was this bloke who lived on my street who went to church every day – a couple of different churches, every day. We thought he was very religious, until he was caught rifling the poor boxes, and that's why he went to church every day. Like I said, it takes all sorts. But that's what makes humans so interesting and keeps us so very busy, isn't it?'

Andy Lukeson came into the DI's office massaging the back of his thigh.

'What happened to you?'

'Slipped on dog poo, just outside,' he groaned. 'Leg went from under me. Pulled something.'

'Next time fall on your head. That way you'll do less damage. Is this team accident prone? First Rochester. Now you. And I hate to bring this up in your war-wounded state, Andy,' Speckle said, 'but you pong.'

Lukeson turned up the sole of his right shoe, which he thought he had rubbed clean on the patch of grass outside the station grandiosely called a garden, and saw the wedge of dog poo between the heel and sole.

'Sorry. Thought I'd got it all.' He stood up to leave. 'Back in a mo.' He grinned. 'Wouldn't want any confusion between dog poo, and your latest perfume, ma'am.'

Sally Speckle took a tissue from a box on her desk and put it daintily to her nose. 'Don't be too long, Andy.'

When he left, Anne Fenning said, 'You two have really hit it off, haven't you?'

Speckle said, 'Yes. Andy Lukeson's a good bloke. And a damn good copper. So, Anne, what's been happening?'

Before she had left for the murder of Melissa Scott, Sally Speckle had given Fenning the task of coordinating the different strands of the investigation which had been forced to take second place to the Scott murder.

When Andy Lukeson came back, Fenning brought her DI and DS up to date.

Speckle summed up: 'It's looking like, so far, that Elinor Roebuck is the most likely candidate to have been the skeleton in that grave.' She explained about the meeting Melissa Scott was to have with Elinor Roebuck in Thatcher's Lot. 'Hers and Finch's dental records are currently being check against the skeleton's teeth.

'Fortunate for us, before Jack Armstrong handed over his practice to Mr Bernstein he made a copy of his patients' records, just in case at some point in the future some legal problem might arise and dates and details would be important.'

The DI consulted WPC Anne Fenning's detailed report on how the different strands of the investigation were progressing, and the only fault she could find with it was Fenning's cramped writing style. Stapled to Fenning's report were reports from DC Charlie Johnson and DC Helen Rochester, bringing her up to date on their lines of inquiry. 'What's all this about –' she screwed up her eyes '– Blackman?'

'Dr Blackman,' Fenning said.

'Who's he?'

'DC Rochester has this idea that Blackman might be involved in some way in the disappearance of Christine Walsh. Blackman is a doctor at Loston Hospital.'

'Where did this Blackman pop up from?'

'He was the doctor who treated Helen at A&E.'

'Evidence.'

'None, really, boss. But Helen thinks it worth pursuing.'

'We've got more than enough on our plate at the moment.' Sally Speckle wasn't sure if she should allow time to be wasted on what was probably a wild goose chase. But she had a high regard for DC Helen Rochester's savvy. 'Not too much time on this, I think,' the DI decided.

She continued her summing up:

'So, working on the premise that it's Elinor Roebuck's

remains we've found, but not entirely ruling out Susan Finch, let's run through the suspects for murder. And first up is David Dees. George 'Pearly' Stevens, that doyen of Loston society, told Helen Rochester that Dees' interest in Elinor Roebuck was the family fortune and she was a way of getting to Emily Roebuck, whom he saw as the better prospect for getting his hands on that fortune, and he succeeded – not in getting the fortune, but in bedding Emily Roebuck.'

'Emily Roebuck?' Lukeson said. 'A bit long in the tooth for Dees, isn't she?'

'A privilege of age is making a fool of yourself, Sarge,' Anne Fenning said. 'My Uncle Harry used to say that. And Uncle Harry made a fool of himself often.'

'According to Stevens, Dees had his work cut out to keep pace with Emily Roebuck,' Speckle said. 'They used to meet at the gym and then have it off in the back of Emily Roebuck's car. But having it off in the back of a car would have its risks. Stevens told Helen Rochester that he could not say if Emily Roebuck ever had Dees to the house for fun and games, but maybe she had? To minimize risk. Or for the sheer comfort.'

'But that would be pretty stupid,' Anne Fenning opined. 'Cyril Roebuck could walk in on them.'

'True,' Speckle agreed. 'But I think Roebuck would have a fairly ordered life that could have been planned around. But not so Elinor Roebuck. She could have walked in on Dees and Mummy in the hay, and feeling naturally vindictive, she might have threatened to blow the whistle on them to Daddy. For Dees, that would have ruled out a route to the Roebuck fortune through Elinor. And if Elinor blew the whistle on them to her father, Dees would have seen his second option of getting his hands on the Roebuck millions slipping from his grasp, because it was likely that Cyril Roebuck would kick his wife out, penniless. All of which makes for a powerful motive for murder for both David Dees and Emily Roebuck, because she stood to lose as much as Dees.'

'But . . .'

'Yes, Anne,' Speckle encouraged Fenning when she hesitated.

'Well, I was only thinking that Dees would have to be a very patient man. To have a chance of getting at Roebuck's money through Elinor Roebuck, he'd have to wait until Emily Roebuck popped her clogs – she'd hardly agree to her lover marrying her daughter, would she? And even then there would be the problem of Cyril Roebuck's agreement to his daughter marrying Dees. Was that likely to happen? And for Dees to get his hands on the Roebuck fortune through Emily, Cyril Roebuck would have had to pop his clogs.'

'Andy, as I recall Cyril Roebuck had a very high colour and very purple lips. Heart trouble, I reckon?' the DI speculated. 'So the wait for Roebuck to pop his clogs may not have been that long, even without, as they say in football, an assist. But with the proverbial hitting the fan, Roebuck would have made certain right away that Emily Roebuck would end up in the poor house. Which meant that Elinor would have to be silenced before she spoke out if Dees wanted to get his hands on Roebuck's money and, equally, Emily Roebuck would have to act quickly to preserve the lifestyle she had become accustomed to.'

'But would Emily Roebuck go along with David Dees killing her daughter, even with the threat of exposure hanging over her?' Anne Fenning questioned. 'And worse, would she kill Elinor herself?'

'Self-preservation is man's oldest instinct,' Andy Lukeson said. 'Desperate times give rise to desperate deeds. And, of course, it would appear that Emily Roebuck was besotted with Dees. And maybe murder wasn't intended. Maybe Elinor Roebuck would not listen to reason and things got out of hand.'

'Liv Benson told us that on the day Elinor Roebuck went missing, her sister Melissa went to Thatcher's Lot to meet her after a phone call that was about David Dees,' Speckle pointed out. 'And that Elinor was in a state. What about Dees? Why had Elinor Roebuck got in a state? Finding Dees in bed with her mother would put Elinor Roebuck in a state, sure enough.

'Another thing, Elinor Roebuck was pregnant. In a rare lucid moment, Jack Armstrong told Charlie Johnson and Sue Blake that she had been worried about any effects a treatement he was carrying out might have on her baby.'

'The bees have been busy while we were away from the

hive,' Lukeson said.

'Which also raises the possibility that whoever made Elinor Roebuck preggers might also have terminated the pregnancy by terminating her.'

'Back to Dees?' Lukeson said.

'Could be,' Speckle answered.

'And Pearly Stevens provided this.' The DI handed her sergeant the black and white photograph of David Dees in drag. 'A very interesting photo, wouldn't you say?'

'Pearly Stevens was being very cooperative,' Lukeson observed.

'DC Rochester can be very persuasive, Andy. You'll note the shoulder-bag with those great brass rings for the strap. Just like the strap that was found in the grave in Thatcher's Lot.'

'Not looking good for Dees, is it?' Lukeson said.

'No,' Speckle agreed. 'That's why you're off to Ireland, Andy.'

'Ireland?'

'The Beara Peninsula in West Cork to be precise. That's where Pearly Stevens says that Dees now lives. I'll arrange for Garda liaison. A grandiose title for the local plod to hold your hand among the natives.

'Now next up is Bernstein. He denied knowing Elinor Roebuck, yet he was seen with her and later had to admit that he had dinner with Elinor in Fandangos. And he also denied knowing Susan Finch until, again, he had to admit that he did.

'Now Finch disappeared on the Saturday night of the afternoon she had called on Bernstein for fun and games after a bust up with her mother Isabella Finch over, guess who? Right – David Dees. Or *Da* Dees as he was fondly known because of his prematurely grey hair.

'And Elinor Roebuck disappeared on the Thursday before Susan Finch did on Saturday. And, according to Bernstein, Elinor Roebuck and Susan Finch were rivals for Dees, and Finch had threatend to *do* Roebuck because of that rivalry. Did she *do* Roebuck? And did she do a runner on Saturday because she had?

'Now, Rachel Bernstein was in Loston when Susan Finch called on her husband. She had a son when she was very young and he turned up some time ago. They meet one Saturday afternoon in the month in Loston – always the third Saturday. Finch would have known this, of course, and it just so happened that when she turned up on Bernstein's doorstep, it was the third Saturday in the month.

'Rachel Bernstein did not come home as usual that Saturday. Bernstein says that she went to the Kimber Theatre on her own, because Bernstein has a problem with confined spaces such as theatres and cinemas.

'He says that it was the small hours of Sunday morning before Rachel arrived home. But what if Rachel in fact came home and heard what was going on upstairs between Bernstein and Susan Finch, slipped out again, and returned to Loston? Went to the Kimber Theatre on

Grey's Quay directly across from the Blue Stocking Club, which at the time was Susan Finch's home from home and, it being a Saturday night, the chances were good that she'd have been there.

'Rachel Bernstein waits until Susan comes out of the Blue Stocking Club, follows her, maybe offers her a lift home, and murders her.

'Bernstein told Charlie Johnson that Rachel hated Susan Finch.'

'Wonder why?' Anne Fenning said cynically.

Andy Lukeson considered the scenario which Sally Speckle had outlined and said, 'The theory has merit, Sally. Bernstein's really dropped himself in it, hasn't he? Remind me if I ever need a dentist to find someone smarter than him.

'Two women that Bernstein knew, but denied knowing, have both gone missing.'

'And there's Fred White, the metal detector man,' the DI said. 'Melissa Scott told her sister that she had seen a man with a metal detector in Thatcher's Lot the day she went there to meet Elinor Roebuck. Melissa waited, but Elinor did not show up.

'But maybe she had shown up, and was already dead.'

'Fred White? Isn't he the man who found the grave?' Fenning asked.

'Yes,' Speckle confirmed.

'But even if White had murdered Elinor Roebuck, he couldn't have buried her surely,' Anne Fenning said.

'Thatcher's Lot isn't a very popular place, but burying a body would be a risky business. A walker or a jogger could pop up from behind a bush any second.'

Speckle said, 'He could have hidden the body and come back later that night to bury it.'

'But what would his motive be?' Fenning asked.

'Elinor Roebuck had the look of a wealthy young woman. Designer clothes. Fred White might have thought her worth robbing. But, frankly, I'd be more inclined towards a sexual motive. Elinor Roebuck was quite a looker. White coming across her alone in the Lot . . . who knows?'

'Check White out, Anne,' Speckle instructed. 'He just might be the needle in the haystack we're looking for.'

'If Fred White is the killer, why would he lead us to the grave?' Fenning wondered.

'By mistake?'

'Mistake?'

'He had mistaken where he had buried her,' Sally Speckle said. 'The metal detector was activated and he instinctively scooped up the earth.'

'Would you have forgotten? I know I wouldn't,' Fenning said. 'Burying a body is not something you forget, is it?'

'The topography of a place like Thatcher's Lot changes all the time, Anne,' Speckle reasoned. 'A tree that had marked the spot a couple of years ago might have been felled or toppled in a storm – the past winter's been particularly windy, trees down everywhere. New growth year on year. Nature reshapes and reinvents all the time.'

'If White had murdered and buried Elinor Roebuck in Thatcher's Lot, wouldn't it be the last place he'd want to be?' WPC Anne Fenning said.

'He might go back,' Andy Lukeson said. 'To check. To see if everything was still hidden.'

'But if he knew where to check, he wouldn't have dug Elinor Roebuck up, would he?' Fenning pondered.

'What if the murder was troubling him? Speckle said. 'What if he thought that by unearthing his secret he wouldn't be suspected of her murder? What the Americans call a pre-emptive strike. The telly is now full of stories about cases twenty and thirty years old suddenly being solved. That must leave a lot of killers waiting for a flashing blue light. Under such circumstances, I think it's reasonable to assume that a murderer might very well return to the scene of his crime to check that everything was all right.

'Might he or she have left some little titbit of forensic evidence at the scene? Something that if found could now be forensically important; something that even a couple of years ago would have been untraceable could now nail him.

'And, of course, there's always the morbid bastard who's fascinated by his crime and returns time and again to relive it.

'And if that's not enough, there's the threat that, due to

the shortage of building land, Thatcher's Lot could be cleared and all its secrets revealed. And, of course, if White acted on impulse, he may have guilt problems. Five years can build up a lot of guilt. Fear and guilt are powerful forces.

'And there's Stevens, of course. All that cooperation might be an effort on his part to move the spotlight away from himself. We know, but could never prove, he dealt drugs. Alf Wright says that his niece Linda got into some dispute with Stevens before she vanished. Pity Wright didn't tell the investigating officers back then. There seems to have been a history of withholding information from the police around that time. So Linda Wright had pissed off Stevens and he dealt with her. Elinor Roebuck might also have gotten into trouble with him. And George 'Pearly' Stevens, I'm sure, would react badly to being threatened.'

'Stevens is a villain,' Lukeson said.

'A very violent villain, Andy.'

'I don't deny that if he thought it necessary he wouldn't off you. But I don't think that Stevens would get involved personally,' Andy Lukeson opined. 'He'd have sent one of his thugs to get his hands dirty.'

'Maybe,' Speckle conceded. 'But murder in Stevens' name is the same as murder by Stevens himself, Andy. And last but maybe not least, there's Cyril Roebuck to be considered. If the skeleton turns out to be that of Linda Wright, it puts him right up there as the prime suspect.

Alf Wright says that on the night she went missing, Linda got into a big posh car, as he described it – black he thinks. Cyril Roebuck has a big posh black car now. Had he back then? Will you check on that, Anne, please?'

'Charlie Johnson is bringing Roebuck in for questioning,' Anne Fenning told Speckle.

'And we've got Simon Scott to question about the murder of his wife Melissa, Andy.'

'They've put him in interview room four,' Fenning said.

'Right.' Sally Speckle pushed back her chair and stood up. 'Rachel Bernstein needs to be interviewed. Fred White and Emily Roebuck, too. Pushed as we are, I'll let you make the arrangements, Anne. You've really proven yourself to be quite an asset in our stretched circumstances.'

'Thank you, boss,' Fenning said, quite chuffed.

'So let's go and find out what Scott has to say for himself, Andy.' She gathered up the files and reports on her desk. 'I'll leave this lot with you, Anne.'

'Oh, there's something else, boss. Probably nothing,' WPC Anne Fenning said. 'Just an oddity that cropped up when I was checking. Emily Roebuck was mugged on the day after Elinor Roebuck went missing.'

A young rookie knocked on the glass door of the office, and Speckle waved him in. 'Fingerprints report, ma'am,' he said, handing over a single sheet report which Speckle glanced at. She thanked the officer, and when he left she informed Andy Lukeson and Anne Fenning:

'The partial on the signet ring Melissa Scott wore is not Liv Benson's or Simon Scott's, and there's no match on the database.'

'The print might not be the killer's at all, of course,' Andy Lukeson said. 'Someone might just have come to the door and shook hands with Melissa Scott. And if it had been Scott's or Liv Benson's it wouldn't have mattered much anyway. A skilful defence QC wouldn't have had much trouble convincing a jury that either could have clasped Melissa Scott's hands, or picked up the ring when she had it off sometime.

'Either Scott or Benson or both could still have murdered Melissa Scott,' DS Andy Lukeson concluded.

CHAPTER SEVENTEEN

Sally Speckle pushed in the door of interview room four in a no-nonsense fashion, pulled out a chair and sat down to face Simon Scott. Scott's brief sat, as all briefs did, face set in stone, though she knew Kenneth Allsop to be a man of an easy-going nature. DS Andy Lukeson pulled out the chair alongside Speckle and, in an equally no-nonsense fashion, sat. The PC present set the video camera in motion. Videoing interviews with suspects was taking over from taped interviews because of undue pressure (true or false) being brought to bear on suspects to confess. Many of these convictions had been successfully challenged. Some may have had right on their side, but most police officers were of the opinion (and a great slice of the public, too) that many of those who had got off on one technicality or another were as guilty as sin, and the general consensus seemed to be that victims of crime were being forgotten about in the legal merry-go-round of protecting the criminal's rights, while the rights of the victimized went down the drain. Interview room four was the only room so far equipped with video. All the other interview rooms still had tape machines. Speckle could not make up her mind about the videoing of interviews, because the process seemed to tar all officers with the same brush.

Of course there were officers who bent the rules to get convictions, but it was the responsibility of senior officers to weed them out and prevent other officers who did things by the book from being maligned because of the actions of a few rogue coppers.

She came straight to the point.

'Did you murder your wife, Mr Scott?'

'No.'

'Did you find your wife's body?'

'Yes.'

'Why did you not inform the police?'

'Have you any idea what it's like to walk in and find your wife murdered?' Scott asked Speckle. 'Your world comes down around you, for God's sake!'

'Does it indeed,' the DI said sceptically. 'You were about to leave your wife for her sister, Mr Scott. To me, I see no reason why your world should come down around you. Unless, of course, when your wife discovered your affair with her sister you feared that your lover would, shall we say' – Sally Speckle's pause was inch perfect – 'take matters into her own hands and have it out with Melissa.'

'Rubbish! Liv wouldn't harm a fly. She'd have done anything for Melissa.'

'Like take her husband from her?'

'Liv and I fell in love. We didn't plan it that way. It just happened. And by then, anyway, both Melissa and I knew that it wasn't ever going to work out for us.'

'OK. You're distraught. In bits at the awful discovery, and informing the police might not have been your number-one priority. But why didn't you phone for an ambulance?'

'Melissa was dead. What good would an ambulance be?'

'How could you be certain that she was dead? Your wife might have only been unconscious. Revivable. Yet you did nothing. And you want us to believe that you did nothing because your world came down around you.'

'Melissa had been stabbed in the heart.'

'How did you know that?' Lukeson pounced.

'It was obvious. She'd been stabbed in the chest. The heart is in the chest.'

'One can be stabbed in the chest without being stabbed in the heart, Mr Scott. But you just said that your wife had been stabbed in the heart. That's very specific. Maybe you knew your wife had been stabbed in the heart because you stabbed her in the heart, Mr Scott?' Andy Lukeson said.

'No. I did not.'

Speckle picked up the questioning. 'Why were you fleeing Loston?'

'Shock. People react differently.'

'Not guilt?'

'If you mean guilt because I had murdered Melissa, Inspector, no. But there were other guilts. The guilt of betrayal, for instance. And the guilt of not having tried harder.'

'We know your wife phoned Loston College, Scott,' Lukeson said. 'Were you aware she had?'

'Yes.'

'So, you know who she spoke to?'

'She didn't speak to anyone. She asked to speak to Robert Callow, but he wasn't available. So she said she'd phone back.'

'Robert Callow?'

'He represents college management on the board of governors.'

'And I take it that Mr Callow would not approve of your relationship with your sister-in-law?'

'Probably not,' Simon Scott admitted quietly.

'What time was that? Shortly after Melissa discovered your treachery, would it be?'

'I suppose. I didn't know she had. Clare, she's the receptionist and switchboard operator at the college, was concerned because Melissa was so distraught. She had offered to get me to the phone, but Melissa said that I was the last person on earth she'd want to speak to. So Clare contacted me in class. I left the college on the pretext of not feeling very well to come home to find out what was wrong with Melissa.'

'The caring husband,' Lukeson intoned, sarcastically.

'Look, Melissa and I had our good times too, you know. It wasn't all bad. In fact, if we'd done one or two things differently, like having a baby when she wanted to, things might have been very different.'

'Do you know what I think, Scott?' Andy Lukeson began. 'I think the purpose of your hurrying home was an exercise in damage limitation that went drastically wrong.'

'I didn't murder my wife!'

'Did you see anyone in the house or outside?'

'No. I wasn't interested in anything but getting to Melissa.'

'*Getting to Melissa,*' Lukeson repeated, putting a world of meaning into the phrase. 'Perhaps your rage made you blind to everything else but doing exactly that, Mr Scott – *getting to Melissa.*'

Scott looked to his brief.

'I believe, Sergeant, that what you're implying by your over-emphasis on my client's words is neither warranted or justified,' Kenneth Allsop said.

'I think that's all for now,' Sally Speckle said.

'Is my client free to go?'

'Not quite yet, Mr Allsop. We may need to speak to him again in a little while.'

The PC switched off the video camera, and then led Scott and his brief out.

'What do you think, Andy? Scott has been pretty up front, hasn't he?'

'Only with information that was in the public domain and easily checked, Sally. He's well built – strong, not your typical teacher type.'

'Stereotype, don't you mean?'

'I suppose. But Scott would have the power to force that knife home, and he was very specific about the knife having gone into the heart. He's a likely bet, Sally.' Lukeson shrugged. 'However, we've had likely bets before who turned out not to be.'

'Buckets of motive,' Speckle said.

'And Liv Benson? It might have happened exactly the same for her if she had got to the flat before Scott. Hot words. Impulsive reaction. But if I had to choose, I'd choose Scott.'

'All we have at the moment is our reconstruction of events as we think they might have happened,' Speckle said. 'Without proof, we won't be able to hold him for long, Andy. And forensics don't have much to offer. Every bit of trace evidence could be legitimately challenged. And the same goes for Benson, because she was a regular visitor to the flat.'

'And, of course, maybe neither Scott nor Benson murdered Melissa.'

'You don't believe that, do you?'

'It's not a matter of what I or we believe, Andy. It's a matter of what we can prove to a sufficient degree to convince a judge and jury. You'd better get yourself over to Ireland to talk to David Dees, Andy.'

'One of the others could go.'

'No. Dees needs to be questioned by someone of your experience and capability.'

Andy Lukeson grinned. 'You'll make my head swim.'

'I've got a half-hour break at three,' said Nurse Crawford of Loston A&E, taken aback by Helen Rochester's invitation to have a drink, which she had thought no more about. It had been the kind of throwaway invitation never intended to be taken up, just a social nicety. 'But, like you, Helen, I can't have a drink on duty.'

'Then coffee and a sticky bun,' Rochester suggested.

'Lovely.'

'There's a café on the corner near the hospital. See you there at, say, three o'clock?'

'Yeah. Three o'clock is fine.'

DC Helen Rochester hung up the phone, and the doubts she had put legs under before making the phone call came charging back on those same legs to haunt her. The theory she had about Christine Walsh's disappearance from the supermarket car park after visiting the oncology clinic at Loston Hospital at that moment seemed off the wall.

At the desk opposite hers, PC Brian Scuttle had his hand under his chin, looking at her with no small degree of pity.

'What?' Rochester snapped.

'If you're wrong there could be a whole lot of shit on the fan,' he warned.

Interview room three had not yet got video recording of interviews, so WPC Sue Blake switched on the tape machine and DC Charlie Johnson recited:

'The time is 4.03 p.m. Present at this interview are: Mr Cyril Roebuck, Ms Sarah Black, Mr Roebuck's solicitor, WPC Sue Blake, PC Ahmed Hussein and DC Charlie Johnson.'

Cyril Roebuck was perspiring profusely, and his colour was worryingly high.

'Are you all right, Mr Roebuck?' was Johnson's first question.

'Yes.'

'Are you sure?'

'Could we get on with this, please,' Roebuck said agitatedly.

'We can postpone and get medical help if—'

'No. The sooner I'm out of here, the sooner I'll be back to my normal self.'

'OK, then,' Charlie Johnson said. 'Mr Roebuck, how

well did you know Linda Wright?'

'Know her?' Roebuck squeaked, his voice breaking. 'I didn't know her at all.'

'So Ms Wright was simply a prostitute you picked up.'

'I didn't pick her up. It was all a misunderstanding. It was raining heavily and I stopped to offer her a lift.'

'A bit risky, isn't it? Offering a woman alone a lift in this day and age?'

'With hindsight, I can see how foolish it was, Constable.'

'Did she accept your offer of kindness?'

'No.'

'She rejected it, then?'

'If she didn't accept it, then she must have rejected it,' Roebuck said brusquely. Then: 'Sorry. All of this is rather distressing for me, you understand.'

Charlie Johnson said ponderously, 'So, just to get the picture straight in my mind, Mr Roebuck. You offered Ms Wright a lift, she refused, and you drove along the street alongside her as she walked on the footpath to persuade her to accept your hospitality? Is that how it was?'

'Yes.'

'But if Linda Wright said no. . . ?'

'I felt sorry for her. She was soaked through, you see.'

'The Good Samaritan, eh?'

'Well, I wouldn't exactly elevate myself to that position,' Roebuck said.

'Neither would I!' Charlie Johnson said.

Cyril Roebuck's colour heightened further. Sarah Black intervened.

'My client is obviously overwrought. Might it not be wise to postpone this interview until he's calmer?'

'It's not our intention to distress your client, Ms Black,' the DC said, and genuinely meant it. 'If Mr Roebuck feels that he can't continue, then by all means we'll postpone the interview.'

Forcing a degree of calmness on himself, Cyril Roebuck said, 'I'd much rather get it over with, Ms Black. Really, I would.'

'If at any time you feel that you can't continue, please say so,' Johnson said.

'I'll be fine.'

Cyril Roebuck filled a glass of water from the pitcher on the table and sipped it.

'Now, Mr Roebuck,' Charlie Johnson continued after a suitable interlude, 'you are claiming that you were trying to help Linda Wright rather than solicit her for sex. Is that correct?'

'Yes.'

'Have you ever picked up a prostitute, Mr Roebuck?'

'No. I'm not that kind of man.'

'Not that kind of man,' Johnson intoned. 'Then I take it that, like Linda Wright in Loston, you were also trying to help the young girl you tried to pick up in Brigham shortly after?'

Cyril Roebuck shook with shock.

'And how many more young girls have you tried to help, Mr Roebuck?'

'They look much older than they are, you know,' he squeaked. 'Must be the kind of life they lead.'

'You like young girls, do you?' Roebuck looked to be on the point of collapse. 'Girls who are really nothing more than children.'

Roebuck's fist hit the table with enough force to spill water from the pitcher. 'They're grown up enough to lead the filthy lives they lead!' he ranted. 'Dirty bitches!'

There was a long tense silence while Roebuck got himself under control.

'They make you angry, do they, Mr Roebuck? These girls?'

Fully under control of his emotions, Roebuck said, 'I don't do anything with these girls, you know. Other than sit and talk.'

'What do you talk about?'

'I try to persuade them to give up their way of life.'

'Have many listened to your wise counsel, Mr Roebuck?' WPC Sue Blake enquired.

'Not really. I'm afraid most of them are lost causes.'

'Calling them dirty bitches is hardly in line with your stated view of wanting to help these girls, is it, Mr Roebuck.' It was a statement, not a question. 'How might you help them? Give them money?'

'Certainly not!'

'Does your wife know you . . . *help* these girls?' Blake pressed.

A sudden fear leapt in Cyril Roebuck's eyes. 'No.'

'Is she not the charitable type, then?'

'Emily wouldn't understand,' Roebuck said, unconvincingly. 'My wife is rather conservative in her views. She'd say that it was their own fault and they should therefore be the ones to get themselves out of the mess they had gotten themselves into in the first place.'

He laughed weakly.

'Emily thinks that social welfare is an incentive for those who should not have been born in the first place to propagate others who should not be born.'

'Radical views indeed,' WPC Sue Blake said, not bothering to hide her contempt. 'So obviously the girls you try to help would be of this social group and therefore unworthy of your . . . consideration?'

'Yes.'

'Well, it's good that someone takes an interest, isn't it?' Sue Blake said, deadpan.

'I try in my small way to help,' Cyril Roebuck said.

'Do you help other young girls, Mr Roebuck?' Charlie Johnson asked. 'Other than prostitutes?'

'I'm not sure I know what you mean.'

'Well, girls you come across in your own circle, for example?'

'If I think I can,' Roebuck said guardedly.

'Most generous,' Johnson said, his tone of voice even

more deadpan than Blake's.

'I don't really understand why I'm here, you know?' Roebuck said.

'You're here,' Johnson said, 'because Linda Wright went missing the night you tried to help her, and the remains found in Thatcher's Lot might be those of Linda Wright.'

Cyril Roebuck grabbed the edge of the table and swayed. 'You can't think that I had anything to do with her murder?'

'Did we say she had been murdered, Mr Roebuck? I don't believe we did.'

'Well, I assumed—'

'Dangerous thing, assumptions,' Charlie Johnson said. He stood up. 'That will be all for now, Mr Roebuck.'

'For now?' Roebuck asked, sounding panicked. 'What do you mean?'

'Just that we may need to talk to you again, in the light of further developments. Interview terminated at 4.25 p.m.'

'Does my wife have to know, about the girls, I mean?'

'Not if she doesn't have to, Mr Roebuck,' Johnson said. 'But, if I were you, in the future I'd probably pick a more traditional charity.'

'Yes. Of course that would be wise.'

'Very wise,' Johnson said.

When she opened the front door, Rachel Bernstein looked

impassively at DC Helen Rochester and PC Brian Scuttle.

'Mrs Bernstein?' Rochester enquired.

'Yes.'

She waited for an explanation for their visit, curiously unperturbed by a visit from the police. Had she been expecting them? Rochester wondered.

'DC Helen Rochester and PC Brian Scuttle.'

Rachel Bernstein still waited for an explanation.

'May we come in?'

Rachel Bernstein hesitated, and Rochester reckoned she was on the point of refusing when she stepped aside. 'The room on your right.'

'Thank you.'

Rochester and Scuttle shared the expensive leather sofa, while Rachel Bernstein occupied a matching armchair. And she continued to wait for an explanation for their visit. Helen Rochester finally gave it.

'We're making enquiries into the disappearance of Susan Finch, Mrs Bernstein,' she said.

'A long time ago.'

'Five years.'

Rachel Bernstein held Rochester's gaze. 'You think that the skeleton found in Thatcher's Lot is her do you?'

'It's one of several possibilities,' Rochester said. 'Do you think it's Susan Finch?'

'If it were, I'd dance for joy.' Rochester and Scuttle were taken aback by Rachel Bernstein's directness. 'And, frankly, it would not be a surprise. Susan Finch was a mischievous whore who destroyed a lot of happiness in a lot of people, and deserved whatever she got.

'But why you're here, I'm not entirely clear on.'

They heard a car arrive, and a minute later Samuel Bernstein strode into the room, his face flushed with fury.

'What do you think you're doing, coming here?' he demanded to know of Rochester.

'Pursuing a line of enquiry, Mr Bernstein,' Rochester said in a calm *I'm not going to be bullied* tone of voice.

'Don't get so het up, darling,' Rachel told her husband. 'If you're afraid that your affair, one of many,' she told Rochester, 'with Susan Finch is about to be revealed, I already know. Have known since the night you took Susan to the folly at the Finches party.'

Rachel Bernstein was quite enjoying her husband's shocked surprise.

'I was the woman with Phillip Finch when you had to – ' her smile was one hundred per cent mischief '– shall we say *withdraw* quickly.'

'You bloody cow!' he exploded.

'Tut, tut, darling. We have guests.'

Bernstein charged out of the room.

'Now what is it I can help you with, Constable Rochester?' Rachel Bernstein asked with an amused smile.

'You were in Loston on the night Susan Finch went missing.'

'Sammy has been telling tales out of school, has he? Yes. It was the third Saturday of the month. And as you no doubt are aware, the third Saturday of every month I meet with Mark, my son.' Her smile lost its amusement and she became sadly reflective. 'I stupidly panicked and gave him up for adoption nineteen years ago. But it could have been worse, because I had contemplated an abortion. And had I gone ahead, the world today would be minus a very kind and loving man.'

'You said you went to a play that night, at the Kimber Theatre?'

'What if I did?'

Rochester played a wild card.

'But you came home first.'

'Did I?' Rachel Bernstein said vaguely. 'I can't really remember, Constable.'

'Odd, wouldn't you say? You seem to have a perfect recollection of that day, except when it comes to whether you came home or not.'

'Well, one comes and goes so often, it all becomes a tiring routine that's easily and quickly forgotten.'

Rochester gambled. 'We have a witness who saw your car turning into the drive here that afternoon.'

'Bless me. Village life can be quite tedious.'

'Does that jog your memory?'

'Not really. But if you say someone saw me turning into my drive, then bully for them. I really can't see what relevance the say-so of this busybody can possibly have.'

'Did you see Susan Finch leave after a visit to your husband?'

'You really are a tenacious thing, aren't you' She laughed. 'No. I did not see her leave. But I did hear them.'

'Hear them?'

'Yes.' Rachel Bernstein pointed to the ceiling. 'Grunting and groaning like pigs in the throes. She – that is, Susan Finch – seemed to think that loud excited screams were part and parcel of sex. I prefer the quieter variety. That way I can let my imagination run riot. So what did I do next, I hear you ask.'

'It would be helpful to know, Mrs Bernstein.'

DC Helen Rochester had a sneaking admiration for Rachel Bernstein. Enjoying a secret life her husband obviously never knew she had, while he thought he had a secret life that she in fact knew everything about.

Funny old world, eh? she thought.

'I left and drove back to Loston. I had an idea in the back of my mind that I'd spend the evening with my son, if he had nothing else to do. I went round to his flat and walked right into his father, my former boyfriend of all those years long ago. My son never said. But on the third Saturday afternoon he met me, and in the evening he met with his father. Apparently his grand plan was to bring the two of us together.'

She smiled fondly.

'He's quite the romantic.'

'And did he?' Brian Scuttle asked, intrigued. 'Bring you together?'

'Yes, but more by mistake than grand design. Alistair,

my son's father, was at the flat when I called,' Rachel said wistfully.

'And this man will verify that you were with him?' Rochester asked.

'If he has to. But he's married now. And he's an innocent bystander in all of this.'

'We'll have to have his name. But if we have to make enquiries, we'll be very discreet.'

'You know, I might at several times have murdered Susan Finch – well, early on, but I didn't. Because I came to realize what an awful shit I was married to.' She gave Helen Rochester the name of her former boyfriend. 'I'm leaving him, you know,' she confided.

'Your husband?'

'Yes.'

'For?'

'God, no. He'd never even contemplate leaving his wife. And frankly I wouldn't want him to. Because after that one night, when all the emotion and nostalgia had been gotten out of the way, I realized that I cared as little for him then as I had previously.

'I had been eighteen. He had been twenty. Ages when all things were possible and the future is so bright that you can't look into it to see the mistakes you could make.

'No, I've secretly bought a house in Portugal and I'm taking my son with me. He wants to be a painter. Just like I wanted to be all those years ago.'

On leaving, PC Brian Scuttle said with no small degree

of admiration, 'What a woman.'

'Yes. What a woman,' DC Helen Rochester agreed.

A woman who, without doubt, had the courage to murder, Rochester reckoned.

CHAPTER EIGHTEEN

'How does anyone live here?' DS Andy Lukeson murmured, as he drove along narrow roads barely the width of the car he was driving, a very modest saloon – 'Sermon' Doyle's last words before leaving had been: 'Don't break the bloody bank when you're over there, Lukeson.' The narrow roads continually twisted and turned, full of deceptive corners that became even narrower once you got into them, and sudden dips and rises that challenged a driver to remain on the road even at a modest sixty kilometres an hour. And if the corners, dips, rises and gullies at either side of the road didn't get you, the surface, having seen little in the way of upgrading since horses and carts had been the main mode of transport, worked hard to do so.

Dark brooding hills were home to a spattering of sheep and goats. The odd colourful farmhouse or cottage indicated the presence of human life, but since he had left Bantry he had only got an occasional glimpse of that life.

The rain did not help.

The village he was headed for had an unpronounceable name and he was depending on a signpost which he could check the name with to get him there. A garda in Bantry had pronounced it for him several times, each time more slowly, and he thought he had got it. But unfortunately five minutes after departing Bantry, the strange-sounding name again became an unintelligible jumble of letters that made no sense.

'I'll phone ahead,' the Bantry garda had said, responding to Lukeson's vague look after he had attempted to direct him. 'The man there will be on the lookout for you. Sure, if things are on the quiet side, he might even come along the road to meet you.'

Andy Lukeson braked at a fingerpost that had the name of the village he was looking for on it. However, the signpost had tilted to an angle so that any one of the three roads leading off the junction could be the one he was looking for, which was no help at all. If he got on to the wrong road, he reckoned that he would be lucky to make it back to Loston nick in time to draw his pension. He was about to take the road which the signpost most favoured when he saw an elderly man riding a bicycle that had been old when he had been a boy.

'Lost, are ya?' the man said, as he drew near, anticipating Andy Lukeson's request for directions.

'I need to get to . . .' He showed the man the piece of paper he had scribbled the name of the village on.

The old man laughed. 'Them kinda names were thought up to confuse your crowd when they were here.'

'I bet it worked, too,' Lukeson said.

'Worked a treat. Gave the Tans a right run round.'

Andy Lukeson's knowledge of Irish history was on a par with all other Englishmen and therefore was practically nil – Irish history and England's role in it not being a subject thought to be of any practical use beyond the talking shop of an Irish pub. But he vaguely recollected that there had been English soldiers in Ireland around the time of the War of Independence called Black and Tans, apparently so called because of the colours of their uniforms – black trousers and tan tunic, he thought, or maybe it was the other way round. He wasn't sure and it did not matter anyway. He assumed that the old man was referring to them. He dared not ask. Englishmen in Ireland instinctively shunned involvement in Irish history and politics.

'But sure all that's behind us now,' the old man said.

Looking around at the lonely and desolate country, Andy Lukeson sincerely hoped it was.

'There's your road,' the old man said, pointing to a road which Lukeson would not have chosen. 'Four miles and you're there.'

Lukeson thanked the old man. He swung on to the road he had indicated. In the rear-view mirror he saw the old man looking after him and Lukeson wondered if, in him, the old man was seeing a latter-day Black and Tan.

Just as he clocked the fourth mile, the village was suddenly in front of him. About midway along the street he saw a parked garda car. He pulled in just beyond the squad car, got out and went to go into the tiny garda station but found it locked.

'Oh, bloody hell!' Andy Lukeson swore. 'All this way and no one at home.'

'Ned will be back in a couple of minutes,' a woman passing told Lukeson. 'He's popped up the street to Mrs O'Leary, an elderly soul who doesn't get out much. If he has the time, Ned runs her out to her brother's place. That's what he's arranging now. I'll drop in on me way and tell him you're here.'

'That's very kind of you,' Lukeson said.

'You're English?' she said, quickly checking the Irish hired car's registration, and by her reaction she did not appreciate what she obviously perceived as a deception.

'Ned is expecting me,' Lukeson said.

'Oh, that's fine then, isn't it,' she said cheerily, and continued on her way to a house further along the street into which she turned. Almost immediately, a tall well-built man came out hurrying along the street towards Lukeson. The worthy Ned no doubt.

'Sorry about that,' Ned said, in an accent that had not a hint of the local in it. 'I'm Ned Cleary, and you must be

Detective Sergeant Lukeson. Bantry told me you were on your way.' He laughed. 'Only I thought you'd take at least a day to find us.'

'It could have taken longer had it not been for an elderly man who fondly recalled the runaround the place names in these parts gave the Tans.'

'That will be the Black and Tans,' Ned Cleary said. 'And the old fellow will be Jack Clancy, who's made it his lifetime's work to remind everyone who'll listen about his father who, according to Jack, was in the Flying Column round these parts, but who in fact spent the time in question working in England and came home when the last couple of shots were being fired to be photographed.'

Ned Cleary laughed again in his easy way.

'No one listens now, of course. But when the Yanks were visiting the old sod in their thousands, Jack Clancy was never short of a pint.'

Cleary's handshake was warm and firm. Andy Lukeson liked Garda Ned Cleary. In fact, had he been a Loston bobby instead of an Irish garda, he reckoned that they would have formed a good friendship and a good partnership.

'You're here to talk to David Dees, right? In connection with some missing woman?'

'Yes.'

'He's very popular round here. Fitted in from the start, and has a pretty good business going for him now.'

'A successful Englishman in Ireland.' Lukeson grinned. 'Whatever next?'

'No taking the piss now,' Clearly laughed. 'Do you want to follow along behind me?' He nodded in the direction of the Garda car. 'Or do you want to jump in?'

'Your car, I think.'

'Righto.' As he drove away, Ned Cleary said, 'Do you think Man U will win the Premiership again this season?'

WPC Anne Fenning ushered Emily Roebuck into DI Sally Speckle's office. Her body language was hostile, as had been her reception of Speckle's phone call an hour before when the DI had suggested that she might prefer to talk at the station rather than at home where Cyril Roebuck might intrude.

'I've nothing to hide, Inspector,' had been Emily Roebuck's reaction.

'Are you quite sure about that, Mrs Roebuck?' Speckle had responded.

An intelligent woman, Emily Roebuck had immediately picked up on the subtext of Speckle's question.

'Perhaps it would be best if I popped along to see you, after all?' she had said.

'I'm sure it would, Mrs Roebuck.'

Emily Roebuck stood just inside the door of Speckle's office, making a statement that she did not intend to stay very long.

'Won't you sit?' Speckle invited.

'I'm in something of a hurry, Inspector.'

'David Dees.'

'What about him?' she asked casually, but there was no hiding the fear in her eyes. DI Sally Speckle's gaze on Emily Roebuck was unwavering. She sat down.

'David and I got involved,' she admitted. 'It's something that I'm not proud of. After the row when he came home with Elinor, I found out where he lived and went to set him to rights. It all got rather heated. I slapped his face. It got more heated, and I tried to slap him again. He caught me by the wrist, we struggled, he kissed me. Next I knew we were on the couch.'

She looked at Speckle.

'David proved himself to be quite an experienced seducer, Inspector. Going to his flat, one of many in an old rambling mausoleum of a house, had its dangers. So David joined my gym, and we'd meet there and then go to my car. Frankly, I couldn't believe what I was doing. David Dees was my first betrayal of Cyril in a very unexciting thirty-five years of marriage.'

All of Emily Roebuck's arrogance had vanished. And despite her previous resentment of that arrogance, Sally Speckle now felt sorry for her. Because underneath all of her arrogance, Emily Roebuck had feet of clay.

'Who told you about David and I, Inspector?'

'That must remain confidential, Mrs Roebuck.'

'Oh, I think I can guess. That toad Pearly Stevens. David' – she said his name in a soft, girlish sort of way –

'warned me that Stevens could be trouble. And he was right. He had us followed. And he—'

'Blackmailed you?' Speckle said, feeling on safe ground to suggest as much, knowing George 'Pearly' Stevens.

'Yes.'

'Is Stevens still blackmailing you, Mrs Roebuck?'

'Yes, he is. But I don't want anything done about it. His demands are not all that much of a drain.'

'You know that Stevens will go on blackmailing you until he'll bleed you dry, don't you?' Speckle warned. 'Maybe you should consider breaking his hold over you by telling your husband, if you're not seeking police intervention.'

Emily Roebuck laughed bitterly.

'Tell Cyril? Oh, God,' she wailed. 'The hypocritical bastard would have me burned at the stake for being what he quaintly calls a loose woman, Inspector.'

'Hypocritical?' Speckle prompted, knowing well Cyril Roebuck's fondness for young girls, hoping for further revelations.

'He can play the whimpering brow-beaten husband so well, can't he?' Emily Roebuck spat, her bitterness intensifying. 'Cyril has perfected the art of inflicting punishment without the visible marks of the less clever torturer. He prefers to scar the mind rather than the body, Inspector. His punishments are subtle and refined, never brutal or uncouth, but they are all the more devastating in their quiet relentlessness.'

Emily Roebuck sat quietly, a dejected figure.

'And he's a pervert, of course. Any young female is fair game for my husband. A predator with a capital P. But not overtly so. Cyril is much too clever and cunning for that.'

She leaned forward.

'There was a young girl, a prostitute, who went missing around the time Elinor did. Her name was Linda Wright. I saw her picture in the paper. Cyril was with her the night she went missing.'

'How do you know this, Mrs Roebuck?'

'I saw him pick her up. At first a police officer scared him off. But he came back. It was my little amusement, Inspector. You see, I could see the signs in Cyril. The restless agitation that marked his longing to indulge his fondness for young girls. So when he'd go out, I'd go upstairs and dress in shabby old clothes that I kept hidden behind the tank in the hot press, and I'd follow him to his haunt. Park the car and walk along the street, watching him in action. In desperation, he tried to pick me up once.'

She laughed giddily.

'I was tempted, Inspector. Just to see the bastard's face when he realized who he had. But I lost courage. Unable to face the inevitable and awful retribution he would visit on me. A coward to the end, you might say.'

DI Sally Speckle regretted having to pile misery on misery for Emily Roebuck, but she had no choice. 'You brought David Dees to the house,' she stated, as if her information was positive rather than guesswork.

'Silly desperation. Being with David made me feel alive, Inspector. He became a drug. I wasn't stupid enough to think he loved me, but I believe he did enjoy me,' she said proudly. 'I, of course, knew that he had a keen eye on the Roebuck money.

'My car was in the garage, and David's, a bright pink one, was too well known around Loston to risk having sex in it. Cyril was on the golf course, which was usually at least a four-hour absence, and Elinor was out with friends. Misfortune befell David and I when Elinor returned unexpectedly and walked in on us. There was the most awful row. Elinor stormed out, threatening to tell Cyril.'

'What would your husband's reaction have been?'

'Oh, he'd have loved it. More grist to his punishment mill, Inspector.'

'Would he have divorced you?'

'No. I don't think so. We'd have gone on, I suppose. We're like that. Nothing as crude as a bust-up. Must keep up appearances at all costs, you see. Show must gone on. The British way, Inspector. At least our version of it.

'Of course he'd have seen that I didn't get a penny of his fortune when he died. When he would no longer have to worry about what people would say.'

'Is Mr Roebuck ill?'

'Ill?'

'I couldn't help noticing his high colour and purple lips

when we were out at the house.'

'How very observant of you, Inspector. Heart. Could pop off at any time.'

'Then might not the shock of your dalliance with David Dees have been bad for your husband, had Elinor told him?'

'Very probably.'

'It might even have caused his death?'

'Indeed it might have,' Emily Roebuck agreed.

'Which would leave you a very rich woman as ... Mrs David Dees, perhaps? One might even think, if one had a suspicious mind, which most police officers have, that Elinor's return home was not as unexpected as it might have been, Mrs Roebuck. In fact it might have been very fortuitous.'

'You mean that David or I or both might have had a hand in Elinor finding us together, Inspector? That the whole fiasco was designed to bring about my husband's demise by shock?'

'It's a thought, Mrs Roebuck.'

'You'll pardon me for saying so, Inspector. But were it the plan to remove Cyril from the scene, it would be a very hit-and-miss method. Don't you think?'

'But if it worked, then it would work beautifully, don't you think, Mrs Roebuck? When did you stop seeing David Dees, Mrs Roebuck?'

'After Elinor went missing.'

'Why was that? Did you think he might have had something to do with your daughter's disappearance?'

'No. I was feeling rather low. So I went round to David's flat.' Her sigh was a weary one. 'David had moved on, another fortune in sight, no doubt. He was in bed with a woman called Susan Finch.'

'Elinor went missing on the day she found you and Dees together, right?'

'Yes.'

'When she stormed out of the house, did you follow her?'

'God, no. She'd have taken my head clean off.'

'Did David Dees follow her?'

'Yes. He thought he'd be able to reason with her.'

'And did he reason with Elinor?'

'Couldn't find her. Said he'd searched high and low.'

'What was his mood? Was he agitated?'

'No. Surprisingly calm, actually.'

'Calm, like he might have solved a problem?'

'David Dees is not a killer, Inspector.'

'You're very sure about that,' Speckle said.

'I am.'

'It was Mr Roebuck who reported Elinor missing. Were you not concerned enough to do so?'

'I thought Elinor had gone off in a huff. She often had before, Inspector. I expected her to walk in the door at any moment.'

'Had that happened, your life could have been over.'

'By then I didn't really give a hang, Inspector. I suppose

I might have been getting to like the idea of not having to live in the straitjacket Cyril had fitted me into a long time ago.'

CHAPTER NINETEEN

DC Helen Rochester was running late, and she feared that Nurse Crawford from Loston A&E would have left, thinking she was not coming. But luckily, she had been delayed also. Having arrived only minutes before Helen Rochester, she had thought that it was Rochester who had left.

'Sorry, I'm late,' Rochester apologized. Crawford had been about to apologize for her lateness, but now let the fault lie with Rochester. 'Coffee and sandwiches OK?'

'Please, my treat, Helen.'

'No. I invited you.'

Being a woman who minded her pennies, Nurse Crawford's protest was a token one. 'I was surprised when you phoned,' she told Rochester when she arrived back with the coffee and sandwiches.

'Why were you surprised?'

'I thought you wouldn't bother.'

'Well, that's frank.'

'I didn't mean that you're ill mannered or shallow,' Crawford said urgently. 'You mustn't think that, please. But you know how it is. "Phone sometime and we'll have a drink," and nothing happens. A throwaway invitation.'

Helen Rochester was having an acute attack of guilt. Crawford had been close to the bone – very close, in fact – because the only reason she had come was to probe Nurse Crawford about Dr Blackman.

Better to make a clean breast of it, she decided.

'Look, I have to be honest with you. I probably wouldn't have phoned—'

'Then why did you?' Crawford asked angrily.

Helen Rochester was surprised by Crawford's anger until, in a flash out of the blue, she understood Crawford's true nature.

'I think there's been some misunderstanding,' Rochester said. 'I'm sorry if you thought—'

'Doesn't matter!'

'Perhaps it would be best if I left.'

'No. I'll go.'

'Look,' Helen said placatingly. 'Why don't we sit and chat and finish our coffee?'

Nurse Crawford began to relax. 'It was my own stupid fault for thinking that you were—'

'It's not important. We can still be friends.'

'Somehow, Helen, I don't think that just being friends

would be possible. Not for me.'

The silence dragged.

'Time for honesty again,' Rochester said, breaking the silence. 'The thing is that I was hoping to ask you about Blackman.'

'What about him?'

'Do you recall that you said he fancied me when he remembered my first name?'

'Yes. Why? Has he—?'

'No.'

'Then I'm not sure I understand, Helen.'

'You also told me that he remembered Christine Walsh's name. Did he fancy her, too?'

Crawford thought for a moment before answering. 'Yes. I believe he did.'

'Would you look at this list for me?' Rochester handed the nurse the list of the missing women. 'And tell me if there's any name on that list, other than Christine Walsh's, that rings a bell.'

Nurse Crawford was shaking her head. Then she stopped. 'Crowe. There was a Mrs Crowe in the oncology ward.'

'When was this?'

'About five and a half years ago, give or take.'

About the time that Alison Crowe had disappeared.

'Her daughter used to visit. I think her name was Alison.'

'Can you check for me?'

'I'll try, Helen.'

'Maybe it would help jog your memory if I faxed you a picture of Alison Crowe?'

'It can't hurt. But I don't understand.'

DC Helen Rochester was tempted to fob Crawford off with the coppers standard get-out: *just routine*. But that would be really mean and underhanded.

'Christine Walsh disappeared from the supermarket car park shortly after leaving the hospital. She walked between a high-sided van and a car and simply vanished. I think she got into the car.'

'Got in? Voluntarily, you mean?'

'Yes. I believe so. Because if she had made even the slightest fuss someone would have noticed. It's a busy supermarket. Whoever was in the car invited Christine to get in and she saw no danger in doing so – someone she trusted. Then the car simply drove out of the supermarket car park and Christine Walsh vanished into thin air. I think it was as simple as that.'

'And you think that this person was Blackman?' Nurse Crawford asked in disbelief.

'That's what I'm trying to find out. I might very well be talking a load of old rubbish, too. But if he also took a fancy to Alison Crowe and she vanished. Well . . And, of course, there's the link to the hospital and Blackman.'

Nurse Crawford was gobsmacked.

'What's Blackman like?'

'I really don't know anything about him. But Mira Long, she's a receptionist at the hospital, says he's weird.'

'In what way?'

'She didn't say. All she said was that going out with him once was one time too many.'

'Can you recall what model of car Blackman had at the time Christine Walsh disappeared?'

'It was white. Biggish.'

Helen Rochester was disappointed. The car at the blindside of the high-sided van in the supermarket car park had been grey according to Sheila, the supermarket employee who had seen it.

'A Mondeo, perhaps?'

'Maybe. But I really couldn't be sure, Helen.'

'Maybe it will come back to you,' Rochester said.

Crawford checked her watch. 'I've got to get back.'

'Thanks for your help. We could have another coffee sometime.'

'I don't think so, Helen,' Crawford said. 'You understand, don't you?'

'Yes. I do.'

' 'Bye.'

'I'll fax you a picture of Alison Crowe within half an hour. What's your fax number?'

'Send it to reception.' She scribbled down the fax number. 'I'll ask Mira to look out for it.'

'Thanks again. I'll see you on Thursday.'

'What?'

Helen Rochester pointed to the dressing over her right eye.

'Day off.'

'Of course, I'd forgotten.'

CHAPTER TWENTY

Garda Ned Cleary took a sharp bend at speed. Andy Lukeson thought that Cleary was probably watching too much telly.

'Just up the lane a bit,' he said.

Lukeson drew back instinctively as the hedgerows on either side of the lane brushed against the windows of the squad car. A short distance on they came to a traditional Irish cottage that might have been lifted from the set of *The Quiet Man*. Cleary braked. The car skidded on the mud, and Lukeson held his breath as the wall of the cottage loomed up. The car stopped inches from it. 'Shite! That was a close call,' Cleary said. He got from the car and knocked on the front door. He got no response, so he called out, 'David! Probably down the field or in the glasshouse,' he confided to Lukeson. He called out again, and David Dees came from behind the cottage. 'Oh, it's there you are,' Cleary greeted Dees. 'Someone here to see you.'

Dees looked at Andy Lukeson and there was a recognition of the species in his glance. 'Let's go inside.'

Lukeson understood now why they called David Dees Da Dees. His hair was completely grey and shoulder length, compared to the short cut he had when a drag artist and DJ at the Blue Stocking Club.

Cleary went to follow, but Lukeson cut his path. The garda proved that he was not slow-witted. 'I'll have a read of the paper in the car,' he said.

Dees led the way through to the kitchen and sat down at the table.

'I've been expecting you,' he said. 'A friend phoned me about the discovery in Thatcher's Lot.'

'I'm DS Andy Lukeson, Loston CID.'

'Is it Elinor Roebuck?'

'We're waiting on the result of dental comparisons. DNA if that doesn't work out.'

'And what is it you want to know from me?' Dees asked. 'I've been through all this before, you know.'

'Certain information has come to light that the investigating officers weren't privy to in the original inquiry and, of course, going over old ground often brings a new perspective.'

'In other words, you think that after five years on I'll trip myself up?'

'It's been known to happen, Mr Dees.'

'So, what's this information you didn't have back then?'

'We know now that you and Emily Roebuck were having an affair. And we also know that Elinor Roebuck, who was the other string to your bow, walked in on you.'

'Pearly Stevens?'

'Yes.'

'Bastard. He's been blackmailing Emily ever since. Did you know that?'

'Yes.'

After her interview with Emily Roebuck, Sally Speckle had phoned Lukeson and brought him up to date.

'Not that I can lay any claim to sainthood. All I had on my mind was getting my hands on the Roebuck millions. Is Cyril Roebuck still alive?'

'He was the last time I heard.'

'Emily said that he could go at any minute. Bad heart. Still around. I'd have had a long wait for riches.'

'Elinor Roebuck stormed out of the house after she found you and her mother together. Emily Roebuck said that you followed to try and reason with her. Is that right?'

'Yes. But I couldn't find her.'

'Did Emily Roebuck leave the house?'

'No.'

'How can you be so sure? She might have left after you, and got back before you.'

'I left her in the bathroom crying. She was there when I

got back, still crying.'

'Elinor was expecting your child, correct?'

'How did you know that?'

'Elinor asked her dentist if some treatment she was having would be harmful to her baby. She rang a friend on the day she went missing. Asked her to meet her in Thatcher's Lot that afternoon. You were the subject of the conversation. Elinor didn't turn up. Were you in Thatcher's Lot that afternoon, Mr Dees?'

'No. I was not.'

'Can you say where you were?'

'Yes. When I got back from searching for Elinor, Emily Roebuck asked me to leave, so I did. I went to see a friend of mine. Spent most of the afternoon with him.'

'And this friend's name would be?'

'Alex Small.'

'And where would I find this friend?'

'You can't.'

'Can't?'

'Dead.'

'Convenient. When did he die?'

'That afternoon. Alex and I were mates growing up. When I was in the shit, which was fairly often, I'd go round and talk to Alex. And that afternoon he did a great deal to set me straight. I told the police where I was, but unfortunately they couldn't check it out.

'When I left Alex, he was leaning over the organ-gallery railings, trying to apply varnish to the rails to save a couple of quid – his church wasn't rolling in it. He fell over the railing. Broke his neck. We were alone. No one saw Alex and me together. So my alibi couldn't be checked.'

'Which means that you have no alibi at all,' Lukeson said.

'That's right. But the police had no proof either. So it was a stand-off.'

'Did you kill Elinor Roebuck?' Lukeson asked.

'No. I did not.'

Lukeson believed him. But there was also Susan Finch to consider.

'I believe that you also knew Susan Finch?'

'Still do, Sergeant.' He called out. 'Susan.' A moment later Susan Finch came into the kitchen. 'Susan is what Alex Small put me straight about. Made me realize how unimportant money is compared to happiness, Sergeant.'

'No one knows I'm here,' Susan Finch said. 'And that's the way I'd like it to be. Just leave me as a missing person.'

'There'll be a police record to set straight. After that your life is yours to do with what you will, Ms Finch.'

When Fred White opened the front door to DI Sally Speckle and WPC Sue Blake, Speckle reckoned that, based on White's sudden pallor, they might have hit the jackpot.

'What do you lot want?' he managed to croak. 'Me and Ettie gave statements, you know.'

'Who is it, Fred?' Ettie White called out from the kitchen, a second before she appeared at the kitchen door. Her reaction on seeing the police was even more stark than her husband's.

'May we come inside?' Speckle asked.

Fred White stepped aside. His pallor now had a grey tinge to it that had aged him twenty years in seconds.

'We've been expecting you,' Ettie White said.

The sharp look which Fred White shot to his wife was rife with panic.

'Oh, we both knew that sooner or later the police would find out, Fred,' Ettie said. She pushed open the sitting-room door. 'Better come in here. I told Fred, you can't get away with something like that, I said. Didn't I say that, Fred? He should have gone to the police there and then – that very afternoon, like I told him to. But no, he thought he could get away with it.'

Sally Speckle turned to Fred White. 'You have something to tell us, Mr White?'

'Yeah. Like Ettie said, I should have talked to you five years ago.'

'I'll never get me new kitchen now, will I?' Ettie White moaned.

Sally Speckle and Sue Blake exchanged puzzled glances, and could not help thinking that worrying about a new kitchen was a very odd thing to be worrying about when your husband was about to confess to murder.

'I'll go upstairs and get it, shall I?' Fred White said.

'Get it?' Speckle asked.

'Yeah. The gold watch I found in Thatcher's Lot.'

'Watch?' Speckle was stunned.

'I know I should have tried to find the owner, it being so expensive an' all. But I reckoned that it would be a little nest egg for later on.'

Having expected a confession of murder, Sally Speckle recovered admirably and speedily to change track.

'Five years ago, you were in Thatcher's Lot when a woman called Elinor Roebuck was there to meet with a friend – the same afternoon she went missing.'

'I don't know nothin' about that,' Fred said, alarmed. 'And who's Elinor Roebuck?'

'Didn't you realize how important finding this watch might be when the police were investigating Elinor Roebuck's disappearance?' Exasperated, Speckle said, 'By not coming forward, Mr White, you could have let a murderer go free.'

'Bloody Moses!' Ettie White wailed.

'Get the watch!' Speckle ordered White sharply.

DC Helen Rochester's fist punched the air on hearing Nurse Crawford's news.

'Yes, Helen, that's a picture of the woman whose mother was in the oncology ward. Blackman used to talk to her a lot. Saw them in a huddle a couple of times. I thought that he was trying to keep Mrs Crowe from hearing bad news. But thinking back now, Alison Crowe was not distressed, as she should have been if it was bad news about her mum.'

'Thanks. I really appreciate you taking the time.'

'There's something else, too. You asked me what car Blackman was driving when Christine Walsh disappeared. Well, it was a grey Mondeo. I remembered that about that time there was a reception at the hospital for the opening of a new wing. A group of us were photographed. Blackman was parking his car and hurried forward to be in the photo. His car is perfectly clear in the picture.'

'You've got it?'

'No. But it's hanging in the staff canteen.'

'Is Blackman on duty now?'

'No, it's his day off.'

'Can you get me Blackman's address?'

'I know it. He lives round the corner from me.'

Sally Speckle took the solid gold watch from Fred White, who was bereft at having to part with it.

'If you'd done what I asked,' Ettie White said, 'they couldn't take away a whole bleedin' kitchen!'

'Oh, shut it, Ettie,' Fred White bellowed. 'There's a name on the back,' he told Speckle.

DI Sally Speckle turned over the watch and saw the name and the inscription:

To Cyril.
On leaving South Africa.

Cyril and Emily Roebuck had lived in South Africa.

CHAPTER TWENTY-ONE

'You're not due back before Thursday, Helen,' Blackman said, his gaze going beyond Rochester to PC Brian Scuttle. 'And I don't see patients at home, I'm afraid.'

'We'd like to talk to you down at the station, Dr Blackman,' Rochester said.

'Oh, dear me. I'm so disappointed. Does this mean that we're not going to be friends?' He considered Helen Rochester with a smug arrogance. 'And, pray tell me, Constable. Why should I accompany you to the station?'

'We want to talk to you about some missing women. Specifically Christine Walsh and Alison Crowe.' Blackman's smugness slipped a little. 'I don't seem to recall the ladies.'

'Let me refresh your memory, then. Both women attended at Loston Hospital. Christine Walsh vanished from the car park of the adjacent supermarket. Only she didn't disappear in the strict sense of the word, did she,

Blackman? Your car, a grey Mondeo, was parked at the blindside of a high-sided van – a white van, actually.'

Little details always made the story and gave it more substance than it really had.

'Christine Walsh was unlucky on the day. She crossed between the high-sided van and your car. You saw an opportunity and grabbed it. You offered Christine Walsh a lift. After her treatment she would have been glad to be offered. And, of course, you were her doctor and a really nice bloke as well. She got in and you drove away. That's how she vanished into thin air.'

Another little bit of Blackman's smug arrogance slipped away.

'I'd have never guessed that inside that pretty head there hid such a fanciful imagination, Constable.' He gave a short, unconvincing laugh. 'You're quite the story-teller. And this other woman, what did you say her name was?'

'I'm sure you don't need me to remind you,' Rochester intoned.

'Proof? Don't you need proof?'

'Oh, we won't have any problem with proof, Blackman,' she said confidently.

DC Helen Rochester hoped that her bluff would convince Blackman that the police could indeed prove what she had accused him of, and what she was now certain to be true. There was a moment when she wasn't sure, when Blackman's smug arrogance re-established itself, but then doubt steadily ate away at it again.

Brian Scuttle stepped forward.

'Please. I do so hate being manhandled.' Blackman's mood became boastful. 'I'd much prefer to do most of this in private, Helen. It will save all that interview-room bother.'

'Where did you find it?' Cyril Roebuck asked Sally Speckle. 'This watch was given to me by friends and it was so precious to me. I thought I'd lost it for ever.'

'It was found in Thatcher's Lot, Mr Roebuck,' Speckle said. 'The afternoon your daughter went missing.'

'I don't understand. How did it get to Thatcher's Lot?'

'I'd suggest that you lost it there when you murdered Elinor,' Speckle said.

'Murdered Elinor?' His astonishment seemed genuine. 'I couldn't murder Elinor. I loved her.'

His final vehemently anguished sentence and its meaning struck DI Sally Speckle. Cyril Roebuck liked young girls, and one of those girls had been Elinor Roebuck.

'Then can you explain how your watch got to be in Thatcher's Lot?' Speckle enquired.

'I don't know.'

'Not nearly good enough, I'm afraid.'

'Inspector, the last time I set eyes on this watch was when I gave it to Emily to take to the jewellers to be cleaned, the day Elinor went missing. But she did not go shopping that afternoon, and the next day she was mugged and the watch was stolen.'

'And the mugger who stole it lost it in Thatcher's Lot? Is that it?'

'Is there another explanation?'

'Oh, yes. I think so, Mr Roebuck,' the DI said. 'Is Mrs Roebuck at home?'

'Emily? Why do you want Emily?'

'Me thinks the game is up, Inspector.' Emily Roebuck strolled into the room and confessed, 'Yes, I murdered Elinor. The mugging was a way out of trying to explain that I'd lost the watch in Thatcher's Lot when I buried Elinor's body.'

'What are you saying, Emily?' Roebuck asked. 'Have you gone barking mad?'

'I was back at the car when I remembered that I had put Cyril's watch in my pocket and it was no longer there. It was a pitch black night. There was nothing I could do. And returning the following day to search did not seem wise. I could only hope that it remained unfound.'

She sighed as if she had lived a thousand years.

'In a way, I'm relieved that it's over.'

'What the devil is going on?' Roebuck asked.

Emily Roebuck's laughter was carefree. 'The skeleton is out of the closet you might say, Cyril. I really did murder Elinor.' Her laughter died. 'No more keeping up appearances,' she said bitterly.

'Having reported a mugging, weren't you worried that whoever found the watch would become a suspect for Elinor's murder?' Speckle asked Emily Roebuck.

'Not in the least. It would probably have been no one of importance. No one that society would have been any the poorer for their loss.'

Sally Speckle was stunned by the woman's total lack of conscience, and lost any sympathy for her.

'How did you kill your daughter, Mrs Roebuck?'

'I strangled her, Inspector. With a strap from David Dees handbag he used in his drag act. He gave it to me as a kind of keepsake. It was ideal. Two great brass strap rings. Remove one, slide the free end of the strap through the other ring and one had the perfect ligature.'

Emily Roebuck had just put into words the unannounced police theory on how the woman found in the Thatcher's Lot grave had been murdered.

'After Elinor found David and I in bed that afternoon, she stormed out of the house and David went after her. But unknown to David, Elinor had simply run round behind the house and had come into the kitchen, where she made a phone call to someone from her mobile phone.

'I had come downstairs with some vague idea of going after David, and overheard Elinor on the phone. It was a conversation that shattered me, Inspector. Elinor was pregnant.' She looked poisonously at Cyril Roebuck. 'By her own father!'

Cyril Roebuck blanched.

'I went back upstairs and prepared the makeshift ligature. Ready, I came down and strangled Elinor. Then I put her body in the boot of my car. That done, I went back upstairs to the bathroom where David had left me crying and where I still was when he got back. He never suspected a thing. Later that night I buried Elinor in Thatcher's Lot.

'As I've explained to you, Inspector. No washing of dirty linen in public. No, that would never do. Not the done thing, you know. So you might say I buried the dirty linen. Socially, it was much preferable to have a missing daughter than one who was pregnant with her father's brat,' she said matter-of-factly.

DI Sally Speckle realized the awful mistake which Emily Roebuck had made.

'Your husband was not the father of Elinor's child, Mrs Roebuck,' she explained. 'It was David Dees.'

'Nonsense. I heard Elinor quite plainly.'

'What exactly did Elinor say, Mrs Roebuck? The exact words, if you can recall.'

'I shan't ever forget, Inspector. Elinor told this person she was on to that she was pregnant and that she was having Daddy's baby.'

'Not Daddy, as in father, Mrs Roebuck. What Elinor was saying was that she was having *Da Dees'* baby. David Dees was called Da Dees by his circle of friends because of his premature greyness. Elinor was having David Dees' baby, Mrs Roebuck.'

Cyril Roebuck sprang at his wife in fury. However, he collapsed before he could reach her. 'Call for an ambulance, Sue,' Sally Speckle told WPC Sue Blake.

Fifteen minutes later Cyril Roebuck was on his way to hospital, but with little or no chance of surviving his heart attack.

Emily Roebuck looked impassively after the ambulance. 'I hope he rots in hell, Inspector,' she said dispassionately.

'Mrs Roebuck, you are under arrest for the murder of Elinor Roebuck. Anything you say—'

'Oh, let's just go, shall we, Inspector!'

Sally Speckle finished the caution. WPC Sue Blake got ready to escort Emily Roebuck.

'Mrs Roebuck . . .'

Emily Roebuck stopped and turned round.

'You didn't only commit one murder, did you?' Emily Roebuck cocked an eyebrow. 'I believe you also murdered a woman called Melissa Scott, a friend of Elinor's from the hectic days of the Blue Stocking Club.'

Emily Roebuck was impassive.

'We found a fingerprint at the scene. On a signet ring Melissa Scott wore. I think that when you shook hands with her, you left your print on the ring, Mrs Roebuck. When we take your fingerprints, I believe we'll be able to match you to the ring.'

Emily Roebuck thought for a moment, before breaking into laughter.

'Do you know what that silly woman did, Inspector? She phoned me to see if I'd mind if she talked to the police. Some nonsense about a meeting she was to have had with Elinor on the day she disappeared; an appointment she had not kept. Well, she couldn't, could she? Elinor was dead. Melissa Scott said she didn't want to upset me by reopening old wounds. She said that she had not told the police at the time about the meeting, because she thought Elinor had just gone off in a huff, something she was prone to do. And that later, telling the police would get her into all sorts of trouble. But now that remains had been found in Thatcher's Lot. Well... I thought it best that she should not talk to the police, Inspector. So, I acted.'

'You drove a knife into her heart!'

'Oh, yes. I work out regularly, so I am strong.'

'Have you no conscience at all?' Speckle asked.

'Conscience? One must do what one must do, Inspector. It's what built an empire.'

'You murdered your daughter for nothing!'

Emily Roebuck thought for a moment. Then, glibly: 'Mistakes happen, Inspector.'

'Sure you won't join me?' Dr Blackman asked DC Helen Rochester and PC Brian Scuttle, swishing the brandy in his glass. Then he laughed. 'Oh, but you're on duty, of course.' He sipped the brandy, strolled to an armchair and sat down. 'So you want to know all about Christine Walsh and Alison Crowe?

'Your recreation of Christine's abduction is inch perfect, Helen, my dear. You might have actually been there. But then if you were, Christine would probably be still alive, or at least she would have been ... *re-rostered*, shall we say. Of the four women I've killed—'

'Four!'

'The fifth, you, dearest Helen, would have been the most stimulating. Pity you didn't get that gash on your head a little earlier.'

Blackman leaned back in the armchair and drank most of the brandy in one swallow. Then he began quite matter-of-factly:

'I became a doctor because I thought it would be easy to satisfy my lust for murder, you see. I've often wondered how many doctors are murderers. When murder can be done so easily, it is rather a difficult temptation to resist, don't you think?

'But I soon found that popping someone off quietly did not quite satisfy me. It lacked that sp[ ] his fingers clutched and unclutche[ ] more personal kind of murder.'

He became animated, his dark e[ ] tory animal's.

'The fight back. The gasping. Th[ ] you relent a little. Then the deliciou[ ] when you snatch back that sliver o[ ] terror of the inevitable takes over.' Blackman's eyes rolled and his body shivered. It took several minutes before he calmed. 'How infinitely exciting real murder is, Helen.'

'You mentioned four women,' Rochester said. 'What

were the names of the other two women?'

'Oh, I think two is enough to be going on with, don't you, Helen darling?' Blackman said. 'One has to keep some little secrets, doesn't one?'

'Where can we find the remains of Christine Walsh and Alison Crowe, then?'

'You really are a trier, Helen. God, how I would have loved to have had you! But like I said, one must keep some little secrets.'

'Bastard!' Rochester said.

EPILOGUE

DI Sally Speckle placed the list of missing women on her desk and drew a line through the names of Elinor Roebuck, Susan Finch, Christine Walsh and Alison Crowe. She looked with a degree of sorrow at the two remaining names from the original list drawn up – those of Ava Black and Linda Wright. 'Do you think Blackman killed Ava Black and Linda Wright?' she enquired of Helen Rochester.

'There's a good chance,' was her opinion. 'Some time in the future he might admit it.'

'Broadmoor's residents tend to keep their secrets, Helen.'

'There's one other idea I had, boss,' DC Rochester said. 'It will need Brian Scuttle to agree. And PC Roger Bennett, too. And we'll need to put a couple of porkies out and about.'

DI Sally Speckle's eyebrows arched.

'Oh, yes. And what would that be?'

*

The man entered the private room at Loston Hospital as quiet as a ghost, glancing back to check the corridor before he closed the door. He looked at the man in the bed, one side of his face covered with a dressing, the other side on the pillow. He was snoring lightly. The man approached the bed cautiously – this man did everything cautiously. On reaching the bed he shook the man gently awake. The man shuffled but did not turn over.

'Pearly Stevens sent me to deliver a message, Bennett,' the man said. 'Pearly says that if you open your trap, he'll have you topped.'

The man was almost to the door of the room, leaving, when it burst open. Helen Rochester and Sally Speckle were accompanied by two burly uniformed officers. The man in the bed, PC Brian Scuttle, sprang out of it to join them, opening his shirt to show his visitor the wire he was wearing. 'Sucker,' he said to the Stevens hardman. 'Believing all that twaddle about Bennett being out of intensive care and about to spill the beans.'

DI Sally Speckle, DCs Helen Rochester and Charlie Johnson, WPCs Anne Fenning and Sue Blake and PC Brian Scuttle were having a celebratory drink in the Plodders Well (officially the King's Head, but because of it being a haunt of off-duty coppers it had come to be known as the

Plodders Well) when DS Andy Lukeson came in.

'A bloke pops over to leprechaun land for a couple of days and you lot put him out of a job,' he complained, grinning.

'What'll you have, Andy?' Sally Speckle asked.

'Champagne, of course, boss.'

'You'll take a pint of Bass the same as the rest, and be glad that you got it!'

Lukeson was just about to put the glass of Bass to his lips when Chief Superintendent Frank 'Sermon' Doyle breezed in. 'The drinks are on me,' he announced. His announcement was intended to include Speckle and her colleagues, but everyone piled up to the bar. 'Bloody hell,' Doyle groaned.

'Everyone got a drink?' Doyle asked ten minutes later. 'Raise your glasses, then,' he instructed. 'And toast the best team in Loston CID. 'And,' he said a moment later, 'now raise them again to the best DI who's come down the line in a long time.'

'Now your problems will really begin, Sally,' Lukeson said. 'They'll expect you to be able to change water into wine.'

Toast finished, the assembled coppers lowered their glasses and broke into applause.

When the excitement quietened down, 'Sermon' Doyle leaned towards Sally Speckle. 'Just a quiet word,' he said. 'Less of the bloody overtime!'

LPLW DISCARD